The Contest of the Singers

By

E. T. A. Hoffmann

British Library Cataloguing-in-Publication Data
A catalogue record for this book is available from the
British Library

Contents

E. T. A. Hoffman

Ernst Theodor Wilhelm Hoffmann was born in Königsberg, East Prussia in 1776. His family were all jurists, and during his youth he was initially encouraged to pursue a career in law. However, in his late teens Hoffman became increasingly interested in literature and philosophy, and spent much of his time reading German classicists and attending lectures by, amongst others, Immanuel Kant.

In was in his twenties, upon moving with his uncle to Berlin, that Hoffman first began to promote himself as a composer, writing an operetta called Die Maske and entering a number of playwriting competitions. Hoffman struggled to establish himself anywhere for a while, flitting between a number of cities and dodging the attentions of Napoleon's occupying troops. In 1808, while living in Bamberg, he began his job as a theatre manager and a music critic, and Hoffman's break came a year later, with the publication of Ritter Gluck. The story centred on a man who meets, or thinks he has met, a long-dead composer, and played into the 'doppelgänger' theme – at that time very popular in literature. It was shortly after this that Hoffman began to use the pseudonym E. T. A. Hoffmann, declaring the 'A' to stand for 'Amadeus', as a tribute to the great composer, Mozart.

Over the next decade, while moving between Dresden, Leipzig and Berlin, Hoffman produced a great range of both literary and musical works. Probably Hoffman's most well-known story, produced in 1816, is 'The Nutcracker and the Mouse King', due to the fact that – some seventy-six years later - it inspired Tchaikovsky's ballet The Nutcracker.

In the same vein, his story 'The Sandman' provided both the inspiration for Léo Delibes's ballet Coppélia, and the basis for a highly influential essay by Sigmund Freud, called 'The Uncanny'. (Indeed, Freud referred to Hoffman as the "unrivalled master of the uncanny in literature.")

Alcohol abuse and syphilis eventually took a great toll on Hoffman though, and – having spent the last year of his life paralysed – he died in Berlin in 1822, aged just 46. His legacy is a powerful one, however: He is seen as a pioneer of both Romanticism and fantasy literature, and his novella, Mademoiselle de Scudéri: A Tale from the Times of Louis XIV is often cited as the first ever detective story.

The Contest of the Singers

At the season when spring and winter are bidding each other farewell--on the night of the Equinox--a reader sat in a lonely chamber with Johann Christoph Wagenseil's work on the glorious craft of the Master Singers open before him. The storm, raging and roaring without, was clearing up the fields, dashing the heavy rain-drops against the windows, and whistling and howling the winter's wild adieu through the chimneys of the houses; whilst the beams of the full moon were dancing and playing like pallid spectres up and down on the wall. But the reader took no note of all this. He closed the book, and gazed, deep in thought, into the fire which was crackling on the hearth, given over wholly to contemplation of the magic forms of long-past times, which his book had evoked for him. It was as if some invisible being laid down veil after veil upon his head, so that the objects around him floated far away into thicker and thicker mists. The raging of the storm and the crackling of the fire turned to gentle, harmonious murmuring whispers, and a voice within him said,

"This is the dream, whose wings murmur so softly up and down, as it lays itself on man's breast like a loving child, awaking with a sweet kiss the inner sight--so that it beholds the beauteous forms of a higher life, which is all splendour and glory."

A dazzling radiance burst forth like lightning-flash, and

the veiled dreamer opened his eyes. But no veil--no mist cloud--now obscured his sight. He was lying on beds of flowers in the twilight dimness of a thick, beautiful forest. The brooks were murmuring, the thickets rustling, like the secret talk of lovers; and between whiles a nightingale complained in sweetest pain. The morning breeze awoke, and--rolling the clouds away--made straight the pathway of the glorious sunshine; and soon the sunlight gleamed upon all the green, green leaves, waking the sleeping birds, which fluttered from spray to spray, singing their joyous strains. Then came sounding from afar the tones of the merry horn. The deer sprang up from their lairs, and the harts and the roes peered out--shyly, with bright, wise eyes--through the leafy thickets, at him who lay on the flowers, and then dashed back in alarm into their coverts again. The horns were silent; but now the chords of harps were heard, and tones of voices, making a music so sweet, that it seemed to come straight from Heaven. Nearer and nearer approached the sound of these beautiful strains, and hunters armed with their boar-spears, with bright horns slung over their shoulders, rode forth from the forest shades. On a splendid cream-coloured charger rode onward a stately lord, dressed in old German garb, robed in a prince's mantle. By his side on a graceful palfrey, a lady of dazzling beauty, richly attired, rode along. After them came six cavaliers, riding on beautiful horses, each of a different colour; their marked and expressive faces spake of a long vanished time. They had laid their bridle reins over their horses' necks, and were playing on lutes and harps, and singing in clear-toned voices. Their horses, trained to the music, went prancing in time to the strains, after the royal pair along the woodland way. When the singing ceased for a time, the hunters sounded their horns, and the horses whinnied and neighed as if in gladness of heart. Pages and servitors richly attired brought up the rear of the stately procession, which wended its way along into the depths of the woods.

He who had been sunk in amaze at this wondrous sight, rose from his flowery couch, and cried enraptured,

"Oh, Ruler of the Universe! have those grand old days arisen again from the grave? What were these glorious forms?"

A deep voice spoke behind him: "Did you not recognize the men, whom you have had so vividly present to your mind?"

He looked round, and saw a grave and stately man in a dark full-bottomed wig, dressed all in black, in the fashion of about the year 1680; and he recognized the learned old Professor Johann Christoph Wagenseil, who went on to speak as follows:

"You need have had no difficulty in seeing that the stately lord in the prince's mantle, was the doughty Landgrave Hermann of Thuringia. By his side rode the star of his court, Countess Mathilda, the youthful widow of Count Cuno of Falkenstein, who died advanced in years. The six who rode after them, singing to lutes and harps, were the six great masters of song, whom the Landgrave--heart and soul devoted to the glorious singer's craft--has assembled at his Court. They are now engaged in the chase; but when that is over, they will meet in a beautiful meadow in the heart of the forest, and hold a singing contest. Thither let us repair, that we may be present when the hunt is over."

Wherefore they went along; while the distant rocks and the woods re-echoed the notes of the horns, the cries of the hounds, and the shouts of the hunters. All turned out as Professor Wagenseil had desired. Scarcely had they come to the gold-green glittering meadow, when the Landgrave, the Countess, and the six masters came slowly up from the distance.

"Good friend!" said Wagenseil, "I shall now point out to you each of the masters, and call him by his name. You see the one who looks about him so joyfully, and, holding his chestnut horse well in hand, comes caracoling up so bravely? The Landgrave nods to him--he gives a happy smile--that is the cheerful, vigorous Walther of the Vogelweid. He with the broad shoulders and the strong, curly beard, with knightly blazon on his shield--riding quietly forward on the piebald--is Reinhard of Zweckhstein. Now, notice him there riding away from us into the woods on a small-sized dapple grey. He gazes thoughtfully before him, and smiles as if fair forms and pictures were rising before him out of the ground; that is the great Professor Heinrich Schreiber. He is probably far away in spirit, and thinks not of the meadow or of the singers' contest. For see how he pushes his way down the narrow woodland path, while the branches above him strike his head.

There goes Johannes Bitterolff after him, that fine-looking man on the sorrel, with the short reddish beard. He calls to the professor, who wakes up from his reverie, and they come riding back together. But what is this wild commotion there amongst the trees; Can storm squalls be passing along down so low in the thickets? This is indeed a wild rider, spurring his horse till he bounds and rears, foaming and fretting. See the pale handsome lad; how his eyes flame, and the muscles of his face are drawn with pain--as if some invisible being were sitting behind him and torturing him--it is Heinrich of Ofterdingen. What can have changed him thus? He used to ride quietly on, joining with beautiful tones in the songs of the other masters. Oh look, now, at this grand cavalier on the white Arab! He is dismounting, and now he swings his bridle reins over his arm, and, with genuine knightly courtesy, holds his hand out to Countess Mathilda to help her from her saddle. See the grace with which he stands, his bright blue eyes beaming on the lady. It is Wolfframb of Eschinbach. But they are taking their places, and the contest is going to begin."

Each of the masters in turn now sung a magnificent song. It was easy to see that they strove to surpass each other. But though none of them did altogether surpass the others--difficult as it was to decide which of them had sung the best--yet the Lady Mathilda bent to Wolfframb of Eschinbach with the garland, which she held in her hand, as the prize. But Heinrich of Ofterdingen sprang up from his seat, with a gleam of wild fire sparkling in his dark eyes; and as he stepped impetuously forward to the centre of the meadow, a gust of wind carried away his barret-cap, and the hair streamed up in spikes on his deadly pale forehead.

"Stay! stay!" he cried, "the prize has not been won! my song, my song has still to be heard; and then let the Landgrave say which of us wins the garland."

"With this there came to his hand--one scarce could tell how or whence--a lute of wonderful form, almost like some strange unearthly creature turned to wood. This lute he began to play and strike with such power, that all the distant woodlands trembled and shook to its tones. Then he sang to its chords in a voice of grandeur and power, in praise of a stranger prince, a mightier prince than all, whom every master must hail and lowly worship, and laud, on pain of shame and dismay, of speedy ruin and end. Often marvellous tones--sneering and harsh, and wild--seemed to sound from the lute, as he was singing this strain.

The Landgrave's glances were angry as this wild singer sang. But the other masters sang all together, joining their voices in answer. Heinrich's wonderful song was well-nigh lost in their singing. So that he swept his strings with more and more passionate swell, till they strained and shivered, and broke, uttering a cry as of pain. Then, in place of the lute, lo! a sudden, dark horrible form was seen to stand at his side; it grasped him with horrible talons, and rose with him up to the air. The songs of the masters ceased, and died away in faint echoes. Black clouds sunk down over forest and meadow, shrouding the scene in night. Then a star arose, shining in soft, gentle radiance, and passed along upon its heavenly way. And the masters floated after this star, resting on shining clouds, singing, and softly touching their strings. A glimmering radiance trembled up from the grass, the woodland voices awoke from their deep slumber, and toned forth, and joined in the masters' songs.

And now you perceive, dear reader, that he who dreamed this dream is he who is about to lead you amongst these masters, to whose acquaintance Professor Johann Christian Wagenseil has introduced him.

Often, when we see strange forms moving in the dimness of distance, our hearts beat with a painful anxiety to know what or whom they may be, and what they are doing. They come nearer and nearer; we can make out the colour of their dress, and see their faces. We hear their voices, although the words cannot be distinguished. But they dip down into the blue haze of some valley, and we can scarcely wait till they come up again and reach us, so eager are we to see them and talk with them, and know what those who seemed so wondrous in the distance may turn out to be when close at hand. May the dream above narrated give rise to similar feelings in you, dear reader, and may you consider that the narrator is doing you no unfriendly service in at once conducting you to the famous Wartburg, and the Court of Landgrave Hermann of Thuringia.

THE MASTER SINGERS AT THE WARTBURG.

It was about the year 1208, that the noble Landgrave of Thuringia, a zealous lover and active patron of the gracious singers-craft, had gathered six mighty masters of song together at his Court. These were Wolfframb of Eschinbach, Walther of the Vogelweid, Reinhardt of Zweckhstein, Heinrich Schreiber, Johannes Bitterolff--all of knightly rank--and Heinrich of Ofterdingen, burgher of Eisenach. The masters dwelt together in heartfelt amity and harmony, as priests of one and the same church, all their efforts being directed to maintaining the gift of song--the most precious wherewith the Lord hath blessed mankind--in full flower and in high honour. Each of them had a "manner" of his own, as it was called, a "style" as we should more probably term it; but just as each note of a harmony differs from all the rest, and yet they all unite in forming the beautiful chord, so the various "modes" or "styles" of these masters harmonized completely together, and seemed but diverse rays of the same star of love. Hence neither of them thought that his own "manner" was the best, but held those of the others in high esteem, and knew that his own "mode" would not sound so beautiful but for the others; just as any note of a chord does not acquire its full beauty, significance, and power until the others belonging to it awake and come lovingly to greet it.

Whilst the songs of Walther of the Vogelweid (a lord of broad acres) were noble and elegantly turned, yet full of exuberant gladness, Reinhardt sung in curt and knightly phrases, employing words and forms of force and might; whilst Heinrich Schreiber was learned and profound, Johannes Bitterolff was full of glitter, and rich in ingenious similes and quaint conceits. Heinrich of Ofterdingen's songs went straight to the depths of the soul. Wasted and worn himself by pain and longing, he knew how to stir the deepest sorrow in the hearts of men; but often there rang through his music harsh accents coming from the torn and wounded breast, where bitter scorn and sorrow had taken their abode, stinging and gnawing like venomous insects. It was a mystery unknown to all why Heinrich had fallen into this condition. Wolfframb of Eschinbach was born in Switzerland, his songs, breathing of grace and peaceful clearness, were like the pure blue skies of his beautiful native land, his "manner" had in it the sounds of the cattle-bells, and of herdsmen playing their reeden pipes; but yet the wild waterfalls lifted their voices, and the thunder among the mountains. As he sang, those who listened were borne floating along with him, on the glittering wavelets of some beautiful stream, now gliding gently, now battling with the storm-driven surges; anon, the storm over, and the danger past, steering in gladness to the wished-for haven. Notwithstanding his youth, Wolfframb of Eschinbach was the most experienced of the masters assembled at the Landgrave's Court. He had been wholly devoted to the singer's craft from his early childhood, and, as soon as he had grown to be a lad, he had travelled in quest of instruction through many countries, till he met with the great master whose name was Friedebrand. This master taught him faithfully in his art, and gave him many master poems in manuscript, which sent light into his inner spirit, enabling him to see and distinguish all that was formless and dim before. More especially at Siegebrunnen, in Scotland, Master Friedebrand gave him certain books from which he learned the histories which he rendered into German song. They related chiefly to Gamurret and his son Parcival, to the Markgrave Wilhelm of Narben and his doughty Rennewart. These poems another master singer, Ulrich of Tuerkheim, afterwards translated into more modern German verse, and enlarged into a thick book at the request of lords and ladies who could not rightly understand Eschinbach's poetry. Thus Wolfframb was renowned far and wide for the excellence of his art, and obtained the favour of many princes and great lords. He visited many courts, and received the richest rewards for his splendid mastership, till at length the enlightened Landgrave Hermann of Thuringia, having heard of his fame from all quarters, invited him to his Court.

Not only his greatness in his art, but his sweet disposition and his modesty, very shortly gained him the Landgrave's fullest favour and affection, and perhaps Heinrich of Ofterdingen, who had formerly enjoyed the full sunshine of the prince's favour had, in consequence, to step somewhat backwards into the shade; but notwithstanding, none of the masters clung to Wolfframb with such sincerity of affection as Heinrich of Ofterdingen. Wolfframb returned it from the depth of his soul; and thus they two stood united in the closest friendship, while the other masters formed a beautiful shining garland around them.

HEINRICH OF OFTERDINGEN's SECRET.

Ofterdingen's wild and distracted condition increased upon him every day; gloomier and more restless grew his glance, paler and paler his cheek. Whilst the other masters, after singing the most sublime themes from holy writ, raised their glad voices in praise of fair ladies, and of their valiant prince, Ofterdingen's songs bewailed the immeasurable pain of earthly existence, and were often like the wailing cry of one who is mortally hurt, and longs in vain for death to deliver him. All believed him to be suffering from hopeless love; but none could succeed in wringing his secret from him. The Landgrave, who was devoted to him heart and soul, tried once, when they chanced to be alone together, to find out the cause of his trouble; he plighted his princely word that he would spare no effort in his power to avert any misfortune threatening him should that be the cause; or, by furthering any desire which might at that time seem hopeless, convert his bitter sufferings into joy and hope; but the Landgrave succeeded no better than the others in inducing young Heinrich to open his heart.

"Alas, my lord!" he said, while the hot tears came to his eyes, "I cannot myself tell what hellish monster has clutched me with fiery talons, and is holding me suspended halfway between heaven and earth. I belong no more to this world; and I thirst in vain for the joys up in the heaven above me. The heathen poets have told of the desolate shades of the dead, who do not belong to Elysium or to Orcus; they flit and wander to and fro on Acheron's banks, and the darksome air, where no star of hope can ever shine, resounds with their cries of sorrow; and the terrible wailings of their inexpressible pain, their weeping, their prayers are vain; the inexorable ferryman drives them away when they try to enter the mysterious barge, and this condition of theirs--this frightful perdition--is mine."

Soon after Heinrich had thus spoken with the Landgrave, he left the Wartburg in a state of real bodily sickness, and betook himself to Eisenach. The masters sorrowed that so fair a flower was lost from their garland, faded before its time, as if by the blight of some poisonous blast; but Wolfframb of Eschinbach by no means gave up all hope--rather he thought that, now that Ofterdingen's mental trouble had turned to a bodily sickness, recovery might be near at hand, for it is not seldom the case that the mind falls sick, presaging bodily pain, and it might be so with Ofterdingen, whom he determined to go and faithfully comfort and tend.

So Wolfframb went at once to Eisenach, and when he went in to Ofterdingen, he found him stretched on his couch, deathly pale, with half-closed eyes; his lute was hung on the wall covered thickly with dust, and many of its strings were broken. When he saw his friend, he raised himself a little, and stretched out his hand to him with a melancholy smile. Wolfframb having taken a seat beside him, and delivered to him the hearty greetings of the Landgrave, and of the other masters; and spoken many other kindly words--Heinrich, in the languid voice of a sick man said, "Much that is strange has happened to me; doubtless I have borne myself as one bereft of his senses. Well might you all believe that some secret, penned up within my breast, was what was driving me so wildly hither and thither; but alas, my wretched state was a mystery even to myself; a raging torture was eating at my heart, but its cause I could not discover. All that I did seemed to me wretched and worthless. The songs which I held so high before, sounded toneless and weak, unworthy the feeblest learner; and yet, befooled by a vain presumption, I burned to outvie you all. A bliss unknown, the highest joy of heaven, shone far above me like a golden star. To it must I raise myself, or perish miserably. I raised my eyes, I stretched my longing arms; but ice-cold wings waved a chill to heart and soul, and a voice said 'What avails thy hope and longing? Is not thine eye blinded? Is not thy power lost? Thou canst not endure the ray of thy hope; thou canst not grasp and hold thy heavenly bliss.' But now, now my secret is plain, even to myself. It is true it gives me my death, but death in the highest of heavenly bliss. Sick and feeble I lay on my bed. It was sometime deep in the night, and the fever-wanderings, which had been driving me hither and thither for so long, left me at once. I felt myself at peace; and a gentle beneficent warmth went spreading through my frame. I seemed to be floating away through the deeps of heaven, borne upon dark clouds. Then a glittering levin-bolt seemed to come cleaving through the gloom, and I cried out--

"'Mathilda! Mathilda!'

"Upon this I awoke. The dream was gone, my heart was

19

throbbing with a strange sweet pain, and with a nameless joy I was conscious that I had cried 'Mathilda,' and I gave way to fear--for I thought that the woods and the meadows, and all the hills and the caves would re-echo that beauteous name--and that thousands of voices would tell her glorious self how deep and true and tender, even to the death, my adoration must always be, and that she is the marvellous star whose beams, streaming into my heart, awake those destroying pains of hopeless longing; and that now those passionate flames have burst into blazing might, that all my soul is athirst, and dies for her peerless beauty!

"You know all my secret now, Wolfframb; bury it deep in your breast. You see that I am peaceful and happy, and you believe me when I tell you that I would rather die than render myself despicable in your eyes--in the eyes of all. But to you--to you, whom Mathilda loves--I felt that I must tell all. As soon as I can rise from this couch, I shall wander away into some foreign land, with death in my heart. Should you hear that I am no more, you may tell Mathilda that I----"

"But Heinrich could speak no further. He sank back upon his couch, and turned his face to the wall. His bitter sobs betrayed the struggle within him.

Wolfframb was greatly startled and surprised at that which Heinrich had disclosed to him. He sat with his eyes fixed on the ground, and considered how his friend might be rescued from the dominion of this mad and foolish passion, which must infallibly lead him to his destruction.

He tried to speak words of comfort, and even to induce

20

Heinrich to go back to the Wartburg, and return--with hope in his heart--into the sunshine which Mathilda shed around her. He even said that it was only by virtue of his songs that he himself had found favour in her eyes, and that Ofterdingen might well reckon upon equal good fortune. But poor Heinrich gazed at him sadly, and said:

"You will never see me, I think, at the Wartburg any more. Would you have me cast myself into the flames? I shall die a happier death afar from her--the sweet death of longing."

Wolfframb departed, leaving Heinrich in Eisenach.

WHAT HAPPENED FURTHER TO HEINRICH OF OFTERDINGEN.

It sometimes comes to pass that the love-pain in our hearts, which at first threatened to tear them asunder, grows habitual after a time, so that we even come to cherish it with care; and the sharp cries of anguish which the nameless torture at first made us utter, turn to melodious plaints of gentle sorrow, which tone back like sweet echoes into our souls, laying themselves, like balm, on our bleeding wounds.

And thus it was with Heinrich of Ofterdingen. His love was as warm and longing as ever, but he looked no more into the black, hopeless abyss. He lifted his eyes to the shimmering clouds of spring, and then it seemed to him as if his beloved was looking down at him with her beautiful eyes, inspiring him with the most glorious songs he had ever sung. He took his lute down from the wall, strung it with fresh strings, and went forth into the fair spring weather which had just commenced. Then he felt powerfully impelled towards the region of the Wartburg; and when he saw the towers of the castle shining in the distance, and reflected that he would never see Mathilda more--that his life would never be anything but a hopeless longing; that Wolfframb had won the peerless lady by the power of song--all his lovely visions of hope sank away into gloomy night, and the deathly pangs of despair and jealousy pierced his heart. Then he fled, as if pursued by evil spirits, back to his lonely chamber, and there he was able to sing songs which brought him delicious dreams, and, in them, the Beloved herself.

For a long time he had succeeded in avoiding the sight of the towers of the Wartburg; but one day he got into the forest--he scarce could tell how--the forest which lies in front of the Wartburg, on going out of which one has the castle close before his sight. He had come to a part of the woods where strangely-shaped crags rise up, covered with many-tinted mosses, surrounded by thick copses and ugly, stunted, prickly underwood. With some difficulty he clambered halfway up these rocks, so that, through a cleft, he could see the towers of the Wartburg rising in the distance. There he sat himself down, and, vanquishing the pain of his gloomy fancies, lost himself in dreams of the sweetest hope.

The sun had been some time set, and from out the gloomy clouds which had come down and spread upon the hill, the moon rose, red and fiery. The night wind began to sigh through the lofty trees, and, touched by its icy breath, the thicket shuddered and shivered like one in the chills of fever. The night birds rose screaming from the rocks, and began their wavering flight. The woodland streams rushed louder--the distant waterfalls lifted their voices. But as the moon begun to shine more brightly through the trees, the tones of distant singing came faintly over the valley. Heinrich rose. He thought how the masters on the Wartburg were now beginning their pious evening hymns. He saw Mathilda, as she retired, casting looks of affection at Wolfframb--whom she loved--with a heart brimming over with fondness and longing. Heinrich took his lute and begun a song such as

23

perhaps he had never sung before. The night wind paused; the thickets and trees kept silence; the tones went gleaming through the woodland shadows as if they were part of the moonlight. But as this song was dying away in sighs of bitter sorrow, a sudden burst of shrill, piercing laughter rang out behind him. He turned quickly round, startled, and saw a tall dark form, which, ere he could collect his thoughts, began to speak in a disagreeable, sneering tone:

"Aha! I have been searching about here for a considerable time to see who might be singing so beautifully at this hour of the night. So it is you, is it, Heinrich of Ofterdingen? Ha! I might have known that, for you are certainly by far the poorest (which is not saying little) of all the 'masters,' as folks call them, up on the Wartburg there; and that silly song, without either meaning or melody, could only have come from your mouth."

Half still alarmed, half glowing in anger, Heinrich cried:

"And who may you be, who know me and think you can attack me here with contumely and scorn?" And he laid his hand on his sword. But the dark stranger gave another of his screaming laughs, and, as he did, a ray of moonlight fell upon his deathly pale face, so that Ofterdingen could see, with much distinctness, the wild-gleaming eyes, the sunken cheeks, the pointed, reddish beard, the mouth with its fixed sneering smile, and the barret-cap with its black feather.

"Heyday, young sir!" said the stranger; "are you going to come at me with lethal weapons because I criticise your songs? I know you singers do not like anything but praise, and expect to receive it for everything that drops from your renowned lips, though there be nothing good about it. But just because that is not my way, and because I tell you candidly that instead of being a master you are but a mediocre scholar and learner of the noble singer's craft, you ought to see that I am your true friend, and mean you kindly."

"How," said Ofterdingen, who felt a secret shudder run through him; "how can you, whom I do not remember to have seen before, be my friend and mean me kindly?"

Without answering this question the stranger went on to say:

"This is a charming spot, and the night is delightful. I will sit down beside you in the friendly light of the moon; you are not going back to Eisenach just yet, so we can have a little chat together. Pay attention to what I am going to tell you, it may prove instructive."

With this the stranger sat down on the large mossy rock, close beside Ofterdingen. The latter struggled with the strangest feelings. With all his fearlessness he could not, in the loneliness of the night, and in that desert place, overcome the profound shuddering which the stranger's voice and manner awakened in him. He felt as if he ought to throw him down the steep precipice into the woodland stream which roared beneath. Then, again, he felt as if paralyzed in all his members.

Meanwhile the stranger came and sat quite close to Ofterdingen and spoke very softly, almost whispering in his ear.

"I have just come from the Wartburg," he said, "where I have been listening to the poor, homely, unskilled, schoolboy-like 'singing,' as it is by courtesy styled, of the so-called 'masters' up there. But the Countess Mathilda is peerless; she is more perfect and charming than any other lady on earth!"

"Mathilda!" Ofterdingen cried in a tone of the deepest sorrow.

"Hoho, young sir," cried the stranger; "it is there where the shoe pinches, is it? However, for the present we have lofty matters to discuss; we have to deal with the noble craft of song. I have no doubt that you people up there mean your best with those songs of yours, and that they all come to you as smoothly and naturally as possible. But of the real, true, profound singer-craft not one of you has the most distant idea. I shall just give you one or two elementary notions on the subject, and then you will see that, on the path on which you are at present, you will never reach the goal you are aiming at."

The dark stranger now began to speak of the true craft of song in very extraordinary language, which itself almost sounded like strange songs hitherto unheard. And as he spoke image after image arose in Heinrich's mind, and then vanished again as if borne away by some storm-wind. A new world seemed to be opening upon him, seething with voluptuous shapes. Each word of the stranger's kindled lightning gleams which flashed forth for an instant and then went out again. The full moon was now high above the trees. Heinrich and the stranger were both sitting in her full radiance, and the former now noticed that the face of the stranger was far from being as horrible as it had appeared at first. There was certainly a strange fire sparkling in his eyes, but Heinrich fancied that a pleasing smile played about his lips, and the great, hawk-like nose and the lofty brow gave the face an expression of immense power and strength.

"I cannot express to you," said Heinrich, "the strangeness of the effect which your words produce upon me. I seem to be only now, for the first time in my life, beginning to form some slight notion what singing really means--as if all that I have done hitherto, under the impression that it was singing, was utterly poor and miserable--and that the true singer's craft was only beginning to dawn upon me. You must certainly yourself be a mighty master of song. Perhaps you will favour me so far as to take me as your most zealous pupil. I most earnestly beg that you will do so."

The stranger gave another of his disagreeable laughs. He rose from his seat and stood before Heinrich, of such giant stature, and with a face so altered, that Heinrich felt the same shudder as when the stranger had first appeared at his side. The latter said, in a voice of such power that it re-echoed amongst the rocks:

"You think I am a mighty master of song, do you? Perhaps I am at times, but the giving of lessons is a matter with which I can by no means be troubled. I have good advice at the service of all who are eager for knowledge, as you seem to be. Have you ever heard of the great master Klingsohr, who is renowned for his mastery of the singer's craft as well as in all other branches of knowledge? People say he is a magician, and has dealings with one who is not everywhere in the best of odour. But do not you be deceived. Things which people do not understand, and cannot themselves manipulate, they think to be supernatural, and pertaining either to Heaven or to Hell. Master Klingsohr will lead you to your goal. His home is in Siebenbürgen; go you to him there, and you will see how science and art have procured for him, in lavish measure, all that his heart could desire--honours and riches, and fair ladies' favour. Ay, my young sir, if Klingsohr were here you would see how little the Lady Mathilda would trouble herself about the gentle Wolfframb of Eschinbach, our sighing Swiss herdsman."

"Do not dare to mention her name!" cried Heinrich. "Begone, and leave me in peace; I shudder at your presence."

"Hoho!" laughed the stranger; "do not get out of temper, my little friend; the cause of your shuddering is the chilliness of the night breeze and the thinness of your doublet. You felt well and happy whilst I was sitting near you, diffusing warmth through your frame. Shuddering and terror! Nonsense! I have blood and fire at your command. As for the Lady Mathilda, what I tell you is that her favour may be gained by means of the singer's gift, such as Master Klingsohr possesses. I began by making light of your singing, to show you your own lack of skill. But the fact that you begin to see your own shortcomings when I give you some inklings of the true craft is sufficient to prove that you are possessed of good dispositions. Who knows? You may be destined to tread in Master Klingsohr's footsteps, and then you may sue for the Lady Mathilda's favour with some reasonable hope of success. So make yourself ready; be off to Siebenbürgen. But stay; if you cannot start off at once I will give you a little book which you shall study diligently. It is a book written by Master Klingsohr, and it contains not only the rules of the true singer's craft, but also one or two admirable compositions of his own."

With this the stranger had produced a little book in a blood-red cover, which glimmered and shone in the moonlight. He handed this book to Heinrich, and, as soon as he had done so, he stepped back and vanished amongst the underwood.

Heinrich fell into a profound sleep. When he awoke the sun was high in the heavens, and, had it not been that the book was lying on his breast, he would have looked upon his adventure with the stranger as merely a vivid dream.

OF THE LADY MATHILDA. EVENTS ON THE WARTBURG.

Doubtless, dear reader, you have at some time or other found yourself in some circle composed of fair ladies and talented men, which might be likened to a fair garland of many-tinted flowers, vieing in colour and perfume. But, like the exquisite tones of a music breathing over the whole, and awaking joy and rapture in every breast, it was the special charm of some one lady in particular, which, outshining the rest of the circle, was the special determining cause of the perfection of harmony pervading the whole. The other ladies seemed more lovely and attractive, seen in the light of her beauty, joining in the music of her voice. It made the men's hearts grow wider, and enabled them to give play to the enthusiasm and inspiration which is shy to come to the light at ordinary times, so that it streamed forth in words or music, or in such form as the nature of the circumstances might suggest. And, however this "queen" of the circle might endeavour, in the kindness and simplicity of her thoughtful goodness and consideration for all, to apportion her favour to each in equal measure, one still could see that her glance singled out one youth in particular standing in silence near her, whose eyes, moist with tears of soft emotion, betrayed the blissfulness of the passion burning in his breast. Many might envy, but none could hate this fortunate being; nay, those who were his friends rather loved him the better for the sake of the love he felt.

"Thus it happened that, in the fair garland of ladies and poets at the Court of Landgrave Hermann of Thuringia, the Countess Mathilda, widow of Count Cuno of Falkenstein (dead at an advanced age), was the fairest flower, surpassing the others in beauty and sweetness.

Wolfframb of Eschinbach, deeply moved by her loveliness and charm, fell in love with her at first sight, and the other masters, inspired by her beauty, celebrated her in many a tuneful lay. Reinhardt of Zweckhstein called her the lady of his thoughts, for whom he was ready to tilt in the tournay, or perish in the fray. Walther of the Vogelweid burned with the most chivalrous passion for her, whilst Heinrich Schreiber and Johannes Bitterolff outvied each other in praising her in every variety of quaint and ingenious conceit. But Wolfframb's songs came from the depths of a loving soul, and found their way to Mathilda's heart like glittering, sharp-pointed arrows. The other masters knew this well, but they felt that Wolfframb's good fortune and happiness irradiated them all with a sunny shimmer, and gave even to their songs a peculiar sweetness and power.

"The first dark shadow that fell upon Wolfframb's radiant life was cast by Ofterdingen's unlucky secret, when he thought how all the other masters loved him, although they, too, were deeply impressed by Mathilda's beauty and grace. As it was only in Ofterdingen's mind that hostile rancour was associated with affection, driving him away into dreary and joyless solitude, he could not help feeling bitterly pained. Often he thought Ofterdingen was only affected by a temporary madness which would wear itself out. Then again he felt with much vividness that he himself would not have been able to endure it if he had sued for Mathilda's favour in vain. "And," he said to himself, "what better claim to it have I? Am I in any way better than Ofterdingen? Am I wiser or handsomer? Where is the difference between us? That which presses him to earth is but the power of a hostile destiny, which might have been mine just as it is his; and I, his faithful friend, pass carelessly by on the other side, and never hold out a hand to help him."

Such reflections brought him at last to the conviction that he must go to Eisenach, and use his utmost efforts to induce Ofterdingen to come back to the Wartburg; but when he arrived Heinrich was gone, no one knew where. Sorrowfully Wolfframb returned to the Wartburg, and told the Landgrave and the masters of Heinrich's disappearance. Then for the first time it was seen how was their affection for him, in spite of his disturbed condition, which was sometimes sullen even to bitterness. They mourned for him as for one dead, and long did this grief lie over all their songs like a gloomy veil, depriving them of all their splendour and tone, till at length the image of the lost one passed further and further away into the dimness of distance.

The spring had come again, and with it all the joy and happiness of renewed life. On a pleasant place in the castle gardens, closed in by beautiful flowers, the masters were assembled to greet the young leaves and the buds and blossoms with festive songs. The Landgrave, with Mathilda and other ladies, had taken their seats in a circle round them, and Wolfframb of Eschinbach was about to begin a song, when a young man, with a lute in his hand, came forward from amongst the trees. With glad surprise they all recognized in him the long missing Heinrich of Ofterdingen. The masters went to meet him with greetings of the heartiest kindliness; but, without taking much notice of them, he approached the Landgrave, to whom, and then to the Countess Mathilda, he made a lowly reverence. He said he was completely cured of the sickness which had been upon him, and begged, should there be any reasons precluding him from being readmitted to the circle of the masters, to be at least allowed to sing his compositions as well as the others. But the Landgrave said that, though he had been away from among them for a time, he was by no means withdrawn from the circle of the masters, and he did not know why he should imagine that that would be the case. He embraced him, and himself pointed out to him his former place, between Walther of the Vogelweid and Wolfframb of Eschinbach. It was soon apparent that Heinrich's looks and bearing were completely changed. Instead of hanging his head as formerly, and creeping about with eyes fixed on the ground, he now walked with a bold firm step, lifting his head on high. His face was as pale as ever, but his glance was firm and penetrating, instead of wavering and uncertain. On his brow, instead of the old deep melancholy, sat a proud, gloomy gravity; and a strange muscular play about his mouth and cheek at times expressed a most uncanny kind of scorn. He deigned no word to the masters, but sat down silent in his place. Whilst the others were singing, he looked at the sky, moved about on his seat, counted on his fingers, yawned--in short, gave every indication of tedium and impatience. Wolfframb of Eschinbach sung in praise of the Landgrave, and then alluded to the return of the dear friend so long absent, describing it so thoroughly out of the depths of his heart that all present were deeply affected. But Heinrich knitted his brows, and, turning away from Wolfframb, took his lute, and struck upon it the most wonderful and extraordinary chords. He advanced to the centre of the circle, and began a song, of which the "manner," wholly unlike anything that the others had sung, was so unprecedented, that every one was struck with the profoundest amazement, and at last consternation. It was as if he was knocking, with tones of might, at the dark portal of some strange mysterious realm, and conjuring forth the mystic secrets of the unknown power therein dwelling. Then he invoked the stars, and his lute's tones whispered soft and low, till one thought one heard the harmonies of the ringing measures of the spheres. Then the chords grew stronger, and rushed louder and louder; and glowing vapours seemed to rise round the assemblage, whilst forms as of voluptuous love-passion glowed in the opened Eden of the pleasures of sense. When he ended all were sunk in the deepest silence, till a burst of applause broke stormily forth; and Lady Mathilda rose quickly from her seat, went up to him, and placed on his brow the garland which she had been holding as the prize.

Ofterdingen's face grew red as fire. He fell on his knees,

and pressed her hands to his breast with rapture. As he rose, his sparkling, penetrating glance fell upon the faithful Wolfframb, who was coming up towards him, but turned away, as if suddenly constrained to do so by some evil power.

There was but one who did not join in the enthusiastic applause, and that was the Landgrave, who had become very grave and thoughtful during Ofterdingen's singing, and could scarce find a word of praise for the marvellous song. At this Ofterdingen seemed visibly annoyed.

When the twilight was almost merging into night, Wolfframb, who had been seeking for Heinrich in vain, met with him in one of the garden alleys. He hastened to him, and after warmly embracing him said:

"Well, dearest brother, and so you have become the greatest master of song, as I suppose, that the world contains. Tell me how you have accomplished what all we others, nay, yourself of old, had not the faintest conception of? What spirit has stood at your command to teach you the marvellous music of another world?"

"It is well," said Heinrich of Ofterdingen coldly, "that you see the height to which I have risen above you, the so-called 'masters'; or rather how I, and I only, have landed, and feel at home, in that realm towards which you are all striving on mistaken paths. You will not blame me, then, for thinking you all somewhat tedious and uninteresting, as well as what you call your 'singing' into the bargain."

"Then," said Wolfframb, "you now altogether despise us, whom of old you held in high esteem--you will have

35

nothing more in common with us. All friendship, all liking have passed away from your heart, because you are a greater master than we. Even me you hold no longer worthy of your regard, because I may not be able to soar as high in my songs as do you. Ah, Heinrich, if I were to tell you what I felt when I heard you sing!"

"Pray let me hear," said Heinrich with a scornful laugh, "perhaps it may teach me something of value."

"Heinrich," said Wolfframb, in a very earnest and serious tone, "it is true your song was couched in a very extraordinary 'manner,' quite unlike anything we had ever heard before, and the ideas soared high, even beyond the clouds. But something within me said that such a song could never come out of the pure human soul, but must be produced by supernatural agency--as necromancers manure the earth of home with magical substances, and it brings forth the strange plants of foreign lands. You have become a great master of song Heinrich, and are occupied in lofty matters; but do you still understand the sweet greeting of the evening wind when you wander through the deep forest shadows? Does your heart still throb with gladness at the rustling of the branches, and the voices of the mountain streams? Do the flowers still look up at you with the eyes of innocent children? Does the nightingale's complaining still make your heart well nigh faint with pain? Ah, Heinrich, there were many things in your song which filled me with a sense of unholy awe. I could not but think of the picture you drew of the poor disembodied shades wandering on the banks of Acheron, when the Landgrave once asked you the cause of your secret pain. I could but fancy that you had bidden farewell to love, and that what you have obtained in its place is but the useless hoard of the wanderer lost in the wilderness. Even now I cannot help fearing--pardon me for speaking so plainly-- that you have bought your mastership with all that joy in life which is only vouchsafed to the pious and childlike of spirit. A dark presentiment seizes me. I think of what drove you from the Wartburg, and the circumstances in which you have returned. Many things may succeed with you, it is true; perhaps the beautiful star of hope to which I have been raising my eyes may set for me for ever. Still, Heinrich--here, take my hand on it--never can any ill-will towards you find place in my heart. Notwithstanding the good fortune which is streaming over you now, should you one day suddenly find yourself on the brink of some deep, bottomless abyss, and the whirl of giddiness seizes you, and you are about to fall down and be destroyed, I shall be standing behind you, firm in heart, and I will hold you fast with my strong arms."

Heinrich had listened in profound silence to all that Wolfframb said. He now covered his face with his mantle, and dashed rapidly in amongst the thick trees. And Wolfframb heard him sighing and gently sobbing as he sped quickly away.

THE CONTEST ON THE WARTBURG.

Much as at first the other masters marvelled at the haughty Heinrich's songs, and praised them, ere long they began to talk of spuriousness in the "manners," of emptiness and superficial display--nay, of absolute wickedness--in the works which he brought before them. Lady Mathilda, and she alone, had turned to the singer with her whole soul; and he praised her charms in a "manner" which all the other masters (except Wolfframb of Eschinbach, who reserved his opinion) declared to be heathenish and abominable. Before very long Lady Mathilda became a wholly altered creature. She looked down upon the other masters with scornful arrogance, and even withdrew her favour from Wolfframb of Eschinbach. She carried matters so far as to ask Heinrich of Ofterdingen to give her instruction in the craft of song, and began to write compositions herself quite in the style of his. From this time all beauty and attractiveness seemed to abandon this poor deluded lady. Discarding everything which serves to adorn noble ladies, and leaving off all womanly ways, she became an uncanny creature, neither woman nor man, detested by the women and laughed at by the men. The Landgrave, fearing that this disorder of hers might infect the other ladies of the Court, issued strict commands that no lady should occupy herself in composition under pain of banishment, and for this the men, who were much horrified at Mathilda's state, thanked him warmly. Countess Mathilda left the Wartburg, and repaired to a castle not far from Eisenach, whither

Heinrich of Ofterdingen would have followed her had not the Landgrave ordered that he should go through with the contest to which the other masters had challenged him.

"Heinrich of Ofterdingen," the Landgrave said to this overweening minstrel, "you have in ugly fashion broken up and disturbed, by those unholy songs of yours, the fair and happy circle which I had collected in this place. Me you could never beguile; I saw clearly, from the beginning, that your songs did not come out of the depths of a pure, honest singer's heart, but were the fruits of the teaching of some false master. What avails outward ornamentation, glitter, and brilliance, when what it covers is merely a lifeless corpse? You sing of lofty matters, of mysteries of the universe, it is true, not as they dawn in the hearts of men, as sweet presciences of a higher life, but as the presumptuous astrologer tries to comprehend them, and reduce and measure them with compass and scale. You should blush, Heinrich of Ofterdingen, to think at what you have arrived, that your brave, honest spirit has bent itself to serve an unworthy master."

"I know not, my Lord," said Heinrich, "how far I merit your displeasure and your reproaches. You may possibly alter your opinion when you hear who the master was who opened to me that province of song which is his own special home. I left your Court in a condition of the deepest melancholy; and it may have been that the pain, which then threatened to destroy me, was in truth only caused by the powerful effort of the germ within me to burst its way towards the fertilizing breath of a higher life. In a strange and remarkable manner a little book came to my hands, in which the greatest master of song on earth had expounded, with the profoundest science, the principles of the art, adding one or two compositions of his own. The more I read and studied in this book, the clearer it became to me what a wretched affair it is when the singer cannot go beyond expressing in words merely that which he fancies he feels in his heart. But, more than this, I felt by degrees as though I were becoming gradually linked on to higher powers, who often sang through me, instead of its being I myself who sang, although I was, in absolute truth, the singer at the same time. My longing to see this great master himself, and listen to the profound wisdom and the critical judgments streaming from his very lips, became irresistible. I went, therefore, to Siebenbürgen, for, pray let me tell you, my Lord, it was to Master Klingsohr himself that I repaired; it is to him I am indebted for the super-earthly scope of my compositions, and perhaps you may now take a more favourable view of my feeble efforts."

"The Duke of Austria," the Landgrave said, "has told and has written me much in praise of your master. Master Klingsohr is versed in profound and secret sciences. He calculates the courses of the stars, and distinguishes the wonderful connection existing between them and the destinies of men. The secrets of the metals, the plants, and the gems are laid open to him, and at the same time he is skilled in the conduct of mundane affairs, and aids the Duke of Austria in action, as well as with advice and counsel. But what all this may have to do with the singer's pureness of heart

I do not know, and I believe, moreover, that this is exactly the reason why Master Klingsohr's music, artfully and cleverly thought out and constructed as it doubtless is, has not the smallest power to touch or move my heart. However that may be, Heinrich of Ofterdingen, my masters, enraged, nay outraged, at your arrogant, overbearing demeanour, desire to sing against you for the prize, for several days together, and that shall now take place."

So the masters' contest began, but whether it was that Ofterdingen's spirit, confounded by false teaching, could no longer find its way by that pure light which served for truthful minds, or whether the interest of the occasion redoubled the powers of the other masters, the result was that each one who sang against him overcame him and gained the prize, in spite of his utmost efforts. Ofterdingen was very angry over this disgrace, and began songs which, with contemptuous allusions to Landgrave Hermann, extolled the Duke of Austria to the skies, calling him the only glorious sun that had arisen upon art. Moreover, he attacked the ladies of the Court with insolent and scornful words, and went on to praise only the charms and beauty of Lady Mathilda, in heathenish and reprobate style. It could not be but that all the masters--the gentle Wolfframb of Eschinbach included--fell into just and righteous indignation at this, so that they trod Heinrich of Ofterdingen's mastership into the mire in the most fervent and unsparing songs. Heinrich Schreiber and Johannes Bitterolff stripped off the false and deceptive outward glitter from Ofterdingen's compositions, and clearly demonstrated the feebleness of the skeleton form hidden beneath. But Walther of the Vogelweid, and Reinhard of Zweckhstein, went further. They maintained that Ofterdingen's conduct was worthy of condign punishment, which they were prepared and eager to inflict upon him, sword in hand.

Thus Heinrich of Ofterdingen saw his mastership contemptuously trodden into the mire, and found even his very life in danger. Full of despair and fury, he appealed to the Landgrave for protection; nay more, to entrust the decision of the contest for the mastership to Master Klingsohr, the most renowned master of the time.

The Landgrave said:

"Matters now have come, between you and the masters, to such a point that it is no longer merely a question of mastership in the singer-craft. In those wild, insane songs of yours you have outraged me, as well as the noble ladies of my Court; therefore my honour and theirs is involved in the question. But it must be decided in singing contest, and I agree to this Master Klingsohr of yours being the arbiter. One of my masters, who shall be chosen by lot, shall contend with you, and the subject you shall treat of shall be left to your own selection. But the headsman shall stand behind you with drawn sword, and he who is vanquished shall be beheaded on the spot. About it, therefore, arrange for Master Klingsohr's arrival at the Wartburg within a year and a day, that he may settle the issue of this trial for life and death."

Heinrich departed, and peace returned to the Wartburg

for the time.

The songs which at this time the masters sang in contest with Heinrich were spoken of as "the war of the Wartburg."

MASTER KLINGSOHR ARRIVES AT EISENACH.

"**Nearly** a year had elapsed when news came to the Wartburg that Master Klingsohr had arrived at Eisenach, and taken up his abode in the house of a citizen named Helgrefe, who lived near the St. George's Gate. The masters were much relieved in their minds that now their bitter quarrel with Heinrich of Ofterdingen would be brought to an end; but none of them was so eager to see this world-renowned master face to face as Wolfframb of Eschinbach. "It may be," he said to himself, "that, as the people say, Klingsohr is devoted to unholy arts, that the powers of evil are at his command, and have aided him to the acquisition of his mastership in all branches of knowledge. But the noblest wine is grown upon congealed lava. What recks the thirsty traveller that the grapes which quench his thirst are nourished by the very fires of hell? I can profit and delight myself by the masters deep knowledge and skilful tuition without asking further questions, only assimilating so much of it as a pure and pious heart may accept."

Wolfframb went off at once to Eisenach. When he came in front of the citizen Helgrefe's house, he found a crowd of people assembled, all staring, in eager expectancy, up at the balcony. He recognized amongst them many young men, scholars of the singer's craft, who kept on quoting this or that saying of the great master. One of them had written down the words he uttered when he went into Helgrefe's house; another knew exactly what he had had for dinner; a third averred that the master had actually looked at him with a smile, because he knew him to be a singer by his barret-cap, which he wore just as Klingsohr did his. A fourth began a song which he said was in Klingsohr's "manner." In short, it was a great excitement and commotion.

Wolfframb of Eschinbach at last succeeded in forcing his way with difficulty through the crowd, and in getting into the house. Helgrefe welcomed him courteously, and, at his desire, went upstairs to announce to the master his arrival. The master, however, was engaged in his studies, and could not receive any one just then. He might come back in a couple of hours. Wolfframb had to swallow this rebuff. He came back in some two hours' time, and had to wait an hour longer. After this, Helgrefe was allowed to usher him in. A strange-looking servant, dressed in silks of many colours, opened the door of the room, and Wolfframb went in. He saw before him a tall stately man, dressed in a robe of dark-red samite, with wide arms, richly trimmed with sable, pacing up and down the chamber with long solemn steps. His face was much like that which classical sculptors have given to their representations of Jupiter, such a domineering gravity sat on the brow, such a formidable fire flashed out of the great eyes. His cheeks and chin were covered by a black curling beard, and on his head was what was either a barret-cap of strange form or a cloth wound round it in a peculiar fashion; it was hard to determine which. He had his arms folded over his breast, and, as he paced up and down, he spoke, in a clear, ringing voice, words which to Wolfframb

45

were incomprehensible. On looking round the chamber, which was full of books and quantities of extraordinary-looking apparatus, Wolfframb saw in one corner a little old pallid mannikin, scarce three feet high, sitting upon a tall stool, busied in writing down, as hard as he could, all that the master was saying, on a leaf of parchment, with a silver pen. When this had been going on for a considerable time, the master's glance fell upon Wolfframb, and, stopping in his walk, he stood still in the centre of the chamber. Wolfframb greeted him with pleasant verses, in a light playful style, explaining that he was come to be edified by Klingsohr's masterly skill and knowledge, and begging him to respond to him in a similar vein, so as to display his powers. The master measured him from head to foot with a wrathful glance, and said:

"Heyday! and who may you be, young sir, who have the impertinence to come here, pitting yourself against me with your idiotic rhymes, as if actually having the overweening presumption to challenge me to a prize-singing? Ah! I see! you can be none other than Wolfframb of Eschinbach, the most unfledged, ignorant laic of those who style themselves masters of the singer's craft up on the Wartburg. No, no, boy! You will have to grow a little ere you can hope to pit yourself against me."

Wolfframb had not looked for a reception of this kind. His blood boiled at Klingsohr's insulting words. He felt the power with which the heavens had gifted him awaking within him more vividly than was usual. He looked the master straight in the eyes, gravely and firmly, and said:

"Master Klingsohr, you do not well in assuming this hard and bitter tone, in place of answering me kindly and frankly, as I addressed you. I know you are my superior in science, and probably also in the singer's craft; but that does not justify you in these arrogant vauntings, which you ought to think beneath you. I tell you to your face, Master Klingsohr, that I now believe that, as the people say, you have power over evil spirits, and intercourse with infernal beings, through the unholy arts which you practise. It is because you can call up dark spirits from the abyss that your mastership is so great. The mind of man stands aghast at them, and it is the terror of them which makes you prevail; not that profound love which streams forth from a pure singer's soul into the heart of the sympathetically-minded. This is why you are arrogant, as no singer, whose heart is untainted, ever can be."

"Hoho!" answered Master Klingsohr, "Hoho, young sir! Do not get on your high horse in this manner. As for my supposed intercourse with powers of evil, be silent. It is beyond your comprehension; it is but the idle chatter of childish idiots that it is from such a source that my skill in sing-craft is derived. But, let me ask you, whence did you derive what small knowledge on the subject you possess? Do you suppose I do not know that at Siegebrunnen, in Scotland, Master Friedebrand lent you certain books, which you, with base ingratitude, did not return, but kept, and that all your songs are taken from them? Ha ha! if I have the devil to thank, you have to thank your own ingrained ingratitude."

Wolfframb was aghast at this horrible accusation. He laid his hand on his heart, and said:

"May God be mine aid!--Amen. The spirit of falsehood is mighty within you, Master Klingsohr. How could I have so shamefully cozened my great master, Friedebrand, of his precious writings? Let me tell you that I kept these manuscripts only just as long as Master Friedebrand wished me to do so, and then gave them back to him again. Have you never learned anything from the writings of other masters?"

"Be that as it may," Klingsohr replied, without paying much attention to what Wolfframb said, "whencesoever you may have derived your art, what warrants you in attempting to place yourself on a level with me? Are you aware how diligently I have studied in Rome, in Paris, in Cracow; that I have travelled to the distant east, and learned the secrets of the wise Arabs; that I have sucked the essence of every school of the singer's craft that exists, and wrung the prize from every one who has competed with me; that I am a master of the Seven Liberal Arts? Whereas you, who have spent your days in far-off Switzerland, at a distance from everything in the shape of art and science, you, who are a mere laic, ignorant of all book-knowledge, cannot by any possibility have acquired even the rudiments of the true craft of song."

During this speech of Klingsohr's, Wolfframb's anger had quite calmed down. The cause may have been that, at Klingsohr's braggart language, the precious gift of song within him shone forth more jubilantly bright, as do the sunbeams when they break victoriously through the heavy clouds which the storm has brought driving up on its wings. A gentle and pleasant smile spread over his face, and he said, in a quiet tone of self-command, to the irritated Master Klingsohr:

'Nay, good master, I might reply that though I have never studied at Rome or Paris, nor sought out the wise Arabs in their own distant land, I have known many singers of fame and skill (to say nothing of my master, Friedebrand, whom I followed into the heart of Scotland) whose instruction has much profited me; and that--like yourself--I have gained the singer's prize at the courts of many of our exalted princes in Germany. But I hold that all instruction, and all intercourse with the greatest masters would have availed me nothing, had not the eternal might of heaven placed within me the spark which has blazed up into the glorious beams of song; had I not held--and did I not still hold--afar from me all that is false or base; did I not strive, with all my strength, to sing nothing other than that which truly fills my heart."

And here he began--he scarcely knew how, or why--to sing a glorious song, in the "Golden Tone," which he had shortly before composed.

Master Klingsohr paced up and down full of wrath. Then he paused before Wolfframb, gazing at him with his fixed, gleaming eyes, as if he would pierce him through and through. When Wolfframb had ended, Klingsohr laid his hands on his shoulders, and said, gently and quietly, "Well, since you will not have it otherwise, Wolfframb, let us sing against one another, in all the tones and manners. But we will go elsewhere; this chamber is not fit for the like. Besides, you must drink a cup of good wine with me."

At this instant the little mannikin who had been writing tumbled down from his stool, and, as he fell hard on to the floor, he gave a little delicate cry of pain. Klingsohr turned quickly round, and pushed the little creature with his foot into a sort of cupboard under the desk, which he closed upon him. Wolfframb heard the mannikin making a low whimpering and sobbing. After this, Klingsohr shut all the books which were lying about open; and each time that he closed one, a strange, awe-inspiring sound, like a death sigh, passed through the room. Next he took up in his hands wonderful roots; which, as he took them, had the appearance of strange unearthly creatures, and struggled with their stems and fibres, as if with arms and legs. Indeed, often a little, distorted human-looking countenance would come jerking out grinning and laughing in a horrible manner. At the same time it grew unquiet in the cupboards round the room, and a great bird appeared, flapping about in wavering, irregular flight with whirring wings that glittered like gold. Darkness was falling fast, and Wolfframb began to feel profound alarm. Klingsohr took a stone out of a case, which immediately diffused a light as bright as the sun through the room. On this all grew still, and Wolfframb saw and heard no more of that which had caused his uneasiness.

Two servants, dressed in the same strange fashion, in many-coloured silks, as the one who had opened the door at first, came in with magnificent garments, in which they dressed their master. And then Klingsohr and Wolfframb went out together to the Town-Cellar.

They drank to friendship and reconciliation, and they sang against each other in all the most skilful and artful "manners." There was no other master present to decide which of them was the victor, but had there been one he would doubtless have declared that Klingsohr had the worst of it. For with the utmost efforts of his art and intelligence he never in the least attained to the power and sweetness of the simple songs which Wolfframb sung.

The latter had just ended one of his most successful essays when Master Klingsohr leaned back in his chair, and said, in a low, gloomy tone:

"You called me vain and braggart, Master Wolfframb; but you would much mistake me if you supposed that I was so blinded by vanity that I should not recognize the true art of song wherever I come across it--were it in the wilderness, or in the master's hall. There is none here to judge between you and me; but I tell you that you have vanquished me Master Wolfframb: and, by my so saying, you may recognize the genuineness of my art."

"Oh, good Master Klingsohr," said Wolfframb, "it may be that a certain special sense of happiness which I feel within me to-night may have made my efforts more successful than they may be at other times. Far be it from me to rank myself higher than you on that account. Perhaps your heart was heavy to-day--how often it happens that a heavy weight seems to lie upon one, like mists resting upon a meadow, and hindering the flowers from lifting up their heads. You may say you are vanquished to-night, but nevertheless I admired much in your beautiful songs, and you may very probably gain the victory to-morrow."

"What does that single-hearted modesty of yours avail you?" cried Master Klingsohr, who started up quickly from his seat, and turning his back to Wolfframb, placed himself at the lofty window, through which he gazed in silence at the pale moonbeams falling from on high.

After some minutes of this he turned, walked up to Wolfframb and said, in a loud voice, while his eyes glared with anger:

"You were right, Wolfframb of Eschinbach. My skill and knowledge are backed up by powers of darkness; and your nature and mine must ever be at variance. You have vanquished me: but in the night which follows this I will send one to you who is called Nasias. Sing against him; and have a care that he does not vanquish you."

With which Master Klingsohr went storming out of the Town-Cellar.

NASIAS COMES BY NIGHT TO VISIT WOLF-FRAMB OF ESCHINBACH.

Wolfframb lodged in Eisenach over against the Bread House with a burgher of the name of Gottschalk: a kindly, pious man who held him in great honour. Although Klingsohr and Eschinbach had thought they were alone and unobserved in the Town-Cellar, it might well have been that many of the young scholars of song who dogged and watched every step of the celebrated master, and strove to catch every word and syllable that fell from his lips, might have found means to listen to the two masters singing against each other. At all events, the news that Wolfframb of Eschinbach had overcome the great Master Klingsohr had spread abroad in Eisenach, so that Gottschalk had come to hear of it. He hastened to his lodger full of joy, and asked him how it could possibly have happened that this haughty master should have consented to undertake a prize-singing in the Town-Cellar. Wolfframb told him all that had happened, not concealing the circumstance that Master Klingsohr had threatened to set one of the name of Nasias at him in the night. At this Gottschalk turned pale with terror, beat his hands together, and cried in a lamentable tone:

"Ah! gracious heavens, good sir, do you not know that Master Klingsohr has dealings with evil spirits, which are subject to him and obliged to execute his commands? Helgrefe, in whose house Master Klingsohr has taken up his abode, tells his neighbours the strangest tales as to what goes on there. It seems that often in the night time one would think a large concourse of people were collected in his room, although no one is ever seen to go in; and then there begins a wild, extraordinary singing, and the strangest goings on of all kinds--all the windows streaming with dazzling light. Very likely this Nasias may be the very evil one in person, and will carry you off to perdition--you ought to set off, dearest master. Do not wait for this terrible visitor--get away, I implore you."

"What?" answered Wolfframb. "My good landlord Gottschalk, why would you have me go away as if I was afraid to sing against this same Nasias? That would not be conduct for a master singer by any means. Be Master Nasias an evil spirit or not, I await him patiently and tranquilly. He may sing me down with his acherontic 'manners,' but he will strive in vain to beguile my pious heart, or to do hurt to my immortal soul!"

"I am well aware," said Gottschalk, "that you are a valiant gentleman, and have not the slightest fear of the very devil himself. But if you are determined to stay here, at least allow my servant Jonas to be in the room with you. He is a pious, stalwart, broad-shouldered fellow, and doesn't mind the singing one hair's breadth. And if you chance to get a little spent, and feel a trifle faint with all the devilish howling--so that Nasias should be like to get the better of you and come at you--Jonas will give a shout, and we will come in with holy water and consecrated candles. And they say the devil cannot endure the stink of musk which a Capuchin friar has worn on his breast in a bag. I'll have some of that handy, and will make such a fumigation that Master Nasias won't have enough breath left to sing a bar."

Wolfframb of Eschinbach laughed at his landlord's kindly anxiety, and said he was now quite ready, and only wished the trial between him and Nasias were over. Jonas, however--the pious man with the broad shoulders, proof against all singing, of whatsoever kind--might stay and be welcome.

"The fateful night arrived. At first all was quiet; till the works of the church clock whirred and rattled, and it struck twelve. Then a gust of wind came breezing through the house, ugly voices howled in confusion and a wild croaking scream as of pain and terror--like that of some frightened night-bird--was heard. Wolfframb had been immersed in beautiful, pure, pious poets' fancies, and had almost forgotten the evil visit in store for him. But now icy shudders ran through his veins; yet he pulled himself together and went to the centre of the room. The door burst open with a tremendous crash, which shook the whole house; and a tall form, surrounded with fiery light, stood before him, and gazed at him with gleaming, malignant eyes. This form was of such terrible aspect that doubtless many a man would have lost his courage, nay, fallen to the ground in wild apprehension; but Wolfframb stood firm, and asked in a grave and emphatic manner:

"What is your will and business in this place?"

The form answered, in a horrible, yelling voice:

55

"I am Nasias, come to contend with you in the singer's craft."

Nasias opened his large cloak, and Wolfframb saw that he had a number of books under his arms, which he let fall on the table beside him. He then at once began a wonderful song, which treated of the Seven Planets and the music of the Heavenly Spheres, as described in Scipio's Dream, and he rang the changes on the most ingenious and complicated "tones" and "manners." Wolfframb, who had seated himself in his armchair, listened calmly, with downcast eyes; and when he had quite finished began a beautiful "tone" or "manner" upon religious themes. At this Nasias jumped hither and thither, and tried to interrupt Wolfframb with howlings, and to throw the heavy books he had brought with him at the singer. But the clearer and the stronger that Wolfframb's song streamed forth, the paler grew Nasias's fieriness, and the more his form crumbled and shrunk together, so that at last he was running up and down on the cupboards, with his little red cloak and the thick ruff at the throat of it, no more than a span long--weaking and squeaking. Wolfframb, when he had ended his song, was going to catch hold of him, but he shot out at once to his original size, and breathed out flames of fire all round him.

"Hei! hei!" he cried, in a terrible voice, "none of these tricks on me, young sir; very likely you may be a great authority on theology, and well versed in the doctrines and subtleties of your fat book; but you are not therefore a singer fit to measure himself against me and my master. Let us have a nice love song, and see where your mastership will be then."

"He then sang a song concerning Fair Helen, and the marvellous delights of the Venusberg. And indeed this song was fascinating; and it was as if the flames which Nasias emitted turned to perfume, breathing voluptuous passion, delight, and desire, amid which the beautiful sounds floated up and down, like love gods at play. Wolfframb had listened to this song as to the former one quietly, with his eyes fixed on the ground. But soon there came to him a sense as though he were wandering along the shady alleys of some beautiful garden, while lovely tones of an exquisite music came floating over the beds of flowers, breaking through the leafy shadows like the dawning red of morning; and the songs of the Evil Thing sunk away before them into night, as the birds of darkness plunge terrified into some deep ravine, croaking at the coming of the day. And as those tones streamed clearer and clearer, his heart throbbed with sweet anticipation and ineffable longing. Soon she who was his life came forth from the thick bushes, in all the splendour of her beauty and grace; and the leaves rustled, and the clear streams plashed, greeting the fairest of women with a thousand sighs of love. She came floating onward, borne on the pinions of song, as on the outstretched wings of a beautiful swan; and when her heavenly glance touched him all the bliss of the purest love-rapture awoke in his heart. In vain he strove to find words, or tones of music. But, when she vanished, he threw himself down on the flowery mead, he called her name to the breezes, he embraced the tall lilies, he kissed the roses on their glowing lips; and all the flowers understood his rapture, and the morning wind, the brooks, and the bushes talked with him of the nameless ecstasy of pure affection.

Thus, while Nasias was going on with his vain and empty love songs, Wolfframb was thinking of the moment when he saw Lady Mathilda for the first time in the garden at the Wartburg; just as she had appeared to him then, he saw her before him now in all her beauty, looking at him with the self-same eyes of love.

"Thus he had heard none of that which the Evil Thing was singing, and when it was done he himself began a song which treated of the bliss of a pious singer's pure affection in the most glorious strains of power.

The Evil Thing grew more and more restless, till at last he began to bleat like a goat, and do all manner of mischief in the room. Then Wolfframb arose, and commanded him, in the name of Christ and the saints, to take himself off. Nasias, spurting out fiery flames around him, gathered his books together, and cried, with mocking laughter:

"Schnib! Schnab! what are you but an ignorant laic?--yield the mastership to Klingsohr!" he stormed out like a hurricane, and a stifling stench of sulphur filled the room.

Wolfframb opened the windows; the fresh morning air streamed in, and cleared away all traces of the Evil Thing. Jonas woke up from the deep sleep into which he had fallen, and wondered not a little to learn that all was over. He called his master, to whom Wolfframb related all that occurred. And if Gottschalk had honoured the noble Wolfframb before, he now looked upon him as a very saint, whose pious power could baffle the denizens of hell itself. When he chanced to cast his eyes towards the ceiling of the room, what was his astonishment to see, written in letters of fire above the door, the words:

"Schnib! Schnab! what are you but an ignorant laic?--yield the mastership to Klingsohr!"

"The Evil Thing had written there the last words he spoke when he took his departure, by way of an eternal defiance. "Not a single happy hour," said Gottschalk, "can I spend in this house while that devilish writing--an affront to my dear Master Wolfframb of Eschinbach--keeps on burning there on the wall." He went off straight and fetched masons to plaster the words over with lime. It was so much labour wasted.

"They put on a finger's depth of lime, and still the writing was as plain as ever. And when they took it all off again and came to the bare bricks the writing was burning upon them as brightly as before. Gottschalk uttered loud complaints, and begged Wolfframb to sing something which should constrain Nasias to remove the horrible writing himself. Wolfframb said, laughing, that this might not be in his power, but that Gottschalk should wait patiently, and see if the writing might perhaps disappear when he had gone away.

It was high noon when Wolfframb of Eschinbach left Eisenach in the happiest possible frame of mind, and the highest spirits, like one who sees the brightest and most hopeful of prospects dawning before him. Not far from the town there came, meeting him, Count Meinhard of Muehlberg, and Walther of Bargel, the cupbearer, dressed in the richest attire, on gaily caparisoned horses, attended by a numerous retinue. Wolfframb saluted them, and learned that Landgrave Hermann had despatched them to Eisenach to escort the renowned Master Klingsohr to the Wartburg. On the previous night Klingsohr had repaired to a high window of Helgrefe's house, and consulted the stars with great care. When he drew his astrological figures, one or two students of astrology, who had joined him, saw from his looks and manner that some important secret which he had read in the stars was filling his mind. They did not hesitate to inquire of him concerning it. Then Klingsohr rose from his seat, and said, in a solemn tone:

"Know that, this night, a daughter will be born to Andreas the Second, King of Hungary. Her name will be Elizabeth; and, for her goodness and virtues, she will be canonized, in after time, by Pope Gregory the Ninth. And this Saint Elizabeth will be the wife of Ludwig, the son of your Landgrave Hermann."

This prophecy was at once communicated to the Landgrave, who was beyond measure delighted thereat. And he altered his opinion concerning the renowned master, whose mysterious knowledge had announced the rising of so fair a star of hope. Wherefore he had determined that Klingsohr should be conducted to the Wartburg with the pomp and ceremony due to a prince.

Wolfframb thought that now, in all probability, the

decision of the singers'life-and-death trial would be postponed on this account, especially as Heinrich of Ofterdingen had not made his appearance as yet. But the knights said that the Landgrave had received news of Heinrich's arrival, that the inner court of the castle was chosen as the scene of the contest, and Stempel, the executioner from Eisenach, ordered to be in attendance.

MASTER KLINGSOHR QUITS THE WARTBURG, AND THE SINGERS-CONTEST IS DECIDED.

In a fair and lofty chamber of the Wartburg sate Landgrave Hermann and Klingsohr in confidential converse together. Klingsohr again assured the Landgrave that he had distinctly seen and carefully read the meaning of the constellations on the previous night, and ended by advising him to despatch an Embassy at once to the King of Hungary to beg that the infant princess might be betrothed to his son, then eleven years of age. This counsel pleased the Landgrave well, and, as he now extolled the master's wisdom, Klingsohr began to discourse so beautifully of the secrets of nature, and of the macrocosm and the microcosm, that the Landgrave (himself not unversed in such matters) was filled with the profoundest admiration.

"Master Klingsohr," said the Landgrave, "I would fain continue in the enjoyment of your skilled and wise society. Leave the inhospitable Siebenbürgen, and take up your abode at this Court of mine, where, as you must admit, Art and Science are more highly prized and more truly cherished than elsewhere. The masters of song will look upon you as their lord, for I make no doubt that you are as highly gifted in their art as in astrology and other profound sciences. Remain here, therefore, and think not of returning to Siebenbürgen."

"Nay," most gracious Prince," said Master Klingsohr, "on the contrary, I must crave your permission to return to Siebenbürgen this very hour. The country is not so inhospitable as you may suppose. And then, it is thoroughly meet for my studies. Consider, moreover, that I may not offend my own king, Andreas the Second, from whom I draw a yearly allowance of three thousand silver marks, on account of my knowledge of mining matters, whereby I have discovered for him many most valuable lodes of metal; so that I live in that peace and freedom which are essential to the due cultivation of science and art. Whereas here--even could I forego my yearly allowance--I should be involved in continual questions and disputes with your masters. My art is based upon other foundations than theirs, and its inward and outward forms are totally different. It may be that their pious minds, and what they term their rich imaginations, suffice to them for the composition of their works, and that, like timid children, they are afraid to enter upon another province of their art. I do not say that I think slightingly of them on that account, but to take my place amongst them is for ever impossible."

"At all events," said the Landgrave, "you will consent to be present, as arbiter and judge, at the great contest between your pupil Heinrich of Ofterdingen and the other masters."

"Your Highness must pardon me," said Master Klingsohr. "How were it possible for me to do this thing? And even were it possible, I should never desire to do it. Yourself, noble Prince, should decide this contest, merely confirming the popular voice, which will assuredly make itself heard. But call not Heinrich of Ofterdingen my pupil. He seemed, at one time, to possess power and courage enough; but he merely gnawed at the bitter shell, and never got so far as to savour the sweetness of the kernel. Fix the day for the contest, therefore; I will take care that Heinrich of Ofterdingen appears with all due punctuality."The most urgent entreaties of the Landgrave were powerless to soften the master's obduracy. He stuck to his resolve, and left the Wartburg laden with rich reward.

The fateful day had arrived on which the singers'-contest was to begin and end. In the castle court lists had been set, almost as if for a tourney. In the centre of the arena there were two seats, draped with black, for the contending singers, and behind them a lofty scaffold. The Landgrave had chosen two noble gentlemen, versed in the singer's craft (they were the same who had escorted Master Klingsohr to the Wartburg), and appointed them arbiters. For them and the Landgrave lofty seats were erected over against those of the contending masters, and beside them were the places for the ladies and other spectators. The masters were to take their places on a bench draped with black, near the contending singers and the scaffold.

Thousands of spectators filled the space, and from all the windows and roofs of the Wartburg an eager throng looked down. The Landgrave, with the arbiters, entered by the castle gate, to the sound of trumpets and muffled drums, and took their seats. The masters, in habits of ceremony, headed by Walther of the Vogelweid, approached, and occupied the seats allotted to them. Upon the scaffold stood Stempel the executioner from Eisenach, with his attendants. He was a gigantic man, of wild, arrogant aspect, wrapped in a wide, blood-red mantle, from the folds of which peeped out the glittering hilt of his enormous sword. Father Leonard, the Landgrave's confessor, took his place in front of the scaffold, to stand by the vanquished in the hour of death.

"A silence of anticipation lay upon the vast assemblage, till the Landgrave's Marshal, wearing the insignia of his office, stepped forward to the centre of the arena, and read aloud the conditions of the contest, and the Landgrave's irreversible decree that he who was vanquished should have his head struck off by the sword. Father Leonard raised the crucifix, and all the masters rose from their seats, and on bended knees vowed, bareheaded, to submit, gladly and readily, to the Landgrave's decree. Stempel then swung his broad, flashing sword three times through the air, and cried, in a voice which echoed through the arena:

"Him who is delivered into my hands I will despatch according to the best of my power and conscience."

The trumpets now sounded; the Marshal advanced to the centre of the arena, and cried aloud, three times running:

"Heinrich of Ofterdingen! Heinrich of Ofterdingen! Heinrich of Ofterdingen!"

"And as though Heinrich had been standing unobserved close to the barriers, waiting till the sound of the Marshal's words should die away, he suddenly stood at his side, in the centre of the arena. He made a lowly reverence to the Landgrave, and said, in a firm voice, he was ready to contend, according to the decree, with the master appointed as his adversary, and to submit to the arbiters' award.

"The Marshal then passed along in front of the masters, holding a silver vase, out of which each of them had to draw a lot. When Wolfframb of Eschinbach unfolded that which he had drawn, he found it marked with the sign indicating that he was the master chosen for the contest. A deadly terror well-nigh unmanned him at the thought of having thus to enter upon a life-and-death contest with his friend. But soon he felt that it was of Heaven's mercy that the lot had fallen on him. If vanquished he would gladly die; but if victor, far sooner would he go to the death than suffer Heinrich of Ofterdingen to perish by the sword of the headsman. With a gladsome heart and a serene and pleasant countenance, he took his appointed place. When he had seated himself opposite to his friend, a strange feeling, akin to fear, took possession of him. For he was certainly looking upon the face of his friend; but out of the deadly pale countenance uncanny eyes were gleaming at him, and he could not help remembering Nasias.

Heinrich of Ofterdingen began his songs, and Wolfframb was greatly startled when he recognised them to be the same which Nasias had sung on the night when he came to him. But he collected himself with all his might, and replied to his antagonist with a magnificent song, in such sort that the acclamations of the thousand voices of the audience rang through the air, and the people at once accorded him the victory. But the Landgrave ordered that Heinrich of Ofterdingen should sing again, and Heinrich went on with songs which, in the marvellousness of their "manners," were so pregnant with the joy of the animalism of life, that the listeners sank into a species of gentle intoxication, as if under the influence of "the drowsy syrups of the East." Even Wolfframb felt himself drawn as into a foreign province of existence. He could think no more of his own songs, nor even of himself.

"At this moment a sound arose at the gate leading to the arena, and the crowd parted and made way. An electric stroke seemed to penetrate Wolfframb; he awoke from his reverie and looked in the direction of this interruption. Oh, Heaven! Lady Mathilda appeared, advancing in all the simple grace and beauty which had adorned her when first he saw her in the Wartburg garden. She looked at him with a glance of the deepest affection; and the blissfulness of heaven and the most glowing rapture soared jubilantly forth in ins song, as had been the case on the night when he vanquished the Evil Thing. With the stormiest enthusiasm the listeners proclaimed him the victor. The Landgrave and the arbiters rose, the trumpets sounded. The Marshal took the garland from the Landgrave's hand to crown the victorious master.

"Then the executioner prepared to do his duty. But when the apparitors went up to seize the vanquished singer, they found themselves grasping at a cloud of black smoke, which rose up, rushing and crackling and suddenly vanished in the air. Heinrich of Ofterdingen had disappeared, none knew how.

The crowd ran wildly hither and thither in confusion, with consternation and terror on their pale faces. People spoke of diabolical forms--of unholy enchantment; but the Landgrave assembled the masters around him, and said:

"I now understand what Master Klingsohr meant when he spoke so strangely and mysteriously on the subject of the singers' contest, and would on no account undertake the deciding of it himself; and I have cause to be grateful to him that all has turned out as it has. Whether it was Heinrich of Ofterdingen who took the place appointed for him in the arena, or one whom Klingsohr sent in his pupil's stead, matters not. The contest is decided in your favour, my trusty masters, and we can now honour the glorious craft of song, and cultivate it to the best of our ability in peace."

Certain of the Landgrave's retainers who had been on warders' duty at the castle said that, at the very time when Wolfframb of Eschinbach won the prize and conquered the ostensible Heinrich of Ofterdingen, a figure much resembling Master Klingsohr had been seen to dash out of the gateway on a foaming steed.

CONCLUSION.

Meanwhile Countess Mathilda had gone into the garden of the Wartburg, and Wolfframb of Eschinbach had followed her.

And when he found her there, seated on a flowery bank of moss, with hands folded in her lap and her lovely head drooping sadly towards the ground, he threw himself at her beloved feet, unable to utter a word. Mathilda put her arms about him, and both of them shed hot tears of sweet sorrow and lovers' pain.

"Ah! Wolfframb," she cried, "what an evil dream has befooled me! How have I, a foolish, unreasoning, blinded child, abandoned myself to the snares of the Evil One who was lying in wait to compass my destruction! Ah! how I have failed in my duty to you! Is it possible that you can pardon me?"

Wolfframb clasped her to his heart, and, for the first time, pressed burning kisses on her rosy lips. He assured her that she had always dwelt in his heart, that he had ever been faithful to her in spite of the powers of evil; that it was she, the lady of his thoughts, alone, who had been his inspiration in the song with which he vanquished them.

"Oh, my beloved!" she said, "let me tell you in what a wonderful manner you rescued me from the snares of the Wicked One which were set for me. There came a night, not very long ago, when strange and terrible ideas took hold upon me. Whether it was bliss or pain that so powerfully oppressed me that I scarce could breathe, I cannot tell. But, driven by an impulse which I could not resist, I began to write a song which was altogether in the 'manner' of my weird master. As I wrote, I heard a strange music, partly beautiful, partly repulsive and horrible, which benumbed my senses, and it was as if, instead of the song, what I had written was some terrible formula, some spell which the powers of darkness must obey. A wild, terrible form started up; it clasped me with burning arms, and was carrying me away to the black abyss. Then a song came shining through the darkness, whose tones had the mild, soft radiance of the light of stars. At this the dark form was compelled to loose its clasp of me, yet it stretched its arms towards me in fury. It could not touch me, but only the song I had been writing. It clutched that, and plunged screaming with it into the abyss. It was your song which saved me, the same which you sung to-day when you won the contest. Now I am wholly yours. My songs are all faithful love for you, whose inexpressible blissfulness no words have power to tell."

The lovers again fell into each other's arms, and could not cease talking of the tortures they had undergone, and the bliss of their reunion.

But in the night when Wolfframb overcame Nasias, Mathilda had distinctly heard, and comprehended--in a dream--the song which Wolfframb, in the height of his inspired affection, was singing; the one which he repeated afterwards at the Wartburg contest.

Wolfframb was sitting in his chamber at late eventide

thinking of new songs, when his landlord Gottschalk came in full of joy, crying:

"Ah! noble sir, how you have vanquished the Evil One by the power of your art and skill! The horrible writing in your chamber has gone out of its own accord, God be praised and thanked for the same! I have brought something which was left at my house to be conveyed to you." With which he produced a folded letter, well sealed with wax. It was from Heinrich of Ofterdingen, and to the following effect.

"I greet you, my trusty Wolfframb, as one who has recovered from some terrible sickness which threatened his death. Many marvellous things have happened to me. But I would fain keep silence as to the evils of a time, which lies behind me now like a dark, impenetrable mystery. Doubtless you remember the words you spoke, when I was boasting of the inward power which elevated me above you and the other masters. You said then, that perhaps I should find myself on the brink of some terrible abyss, a prey to giddiness, ready to fall down into it; and that then you would hold me back with your strong arms. Wolfframb, that which your prophetic soul foresaw, was that which came to pass! I stood on the brink of an abyss, and you held me fast when the fatal giddiness had wellnigh benumbed my senses. It was your splendid victory which annihilated my adversary, and restored me to life and happiness. Yes, Wolfframb! before your love the mighty veils which enwrapped me fell away, and I looked up again to the bright heavens. Can my affection for you be otherwise than redoubled? You recognized Klingsohr as a great master--

and that he is. But woe to him who--not endowed with that peculiar strength which he possesses--ventures, like him, to strive towards the dark realm, which he has laid open to himself. I have renounced him, and totter on the brink of the Hell-river, helpless and wretched, no longer. I am restored to the joys of home.

"Mathilda, ah no! Doubtless it was never that glorious lady. It was some foul enchantment, which filled me with deceptive visions of a paradise on earth--of vain, mundane pleasure. May all that I did in my days of madness be forgotten. Greet the masters, and tell them how it is with me now. Fare thee well, most sincerely beloved Wolfframb. Peradventure you may hear tidings of me ere long."

After some time news came to the Wartburg that Heinrich was at the Court of Leopold the Seventh, Duke of Austria, singing many beautiful songs. Soon afterwards Landgrave Hermann received copies of the same, together with the "manners" to which they were to be sung. All the masters were heartily delighted, and convinced that Heinrich of Ofterdingen had renounced all that was false, and preserved his pure singer's heart inviolate, through all the Evil One's attempts upon him.

Thus it was Wolfframb of Eschinbach's high art of song, as it streamed from the depths of his purest of souls, which, in glorious victory over his enemy, rescued his beloved and his friend from utter perdition.'"

The friends gave diverse verdicts as to Cyprian's tale,

Theodore disapproved of it altogether, and said Cyprian had utterly marred for him the beautiful picture, which Novalis had drawn of the grandly inspired Heinrich of Ofterdingen. But his chief objection was that the singers never actually got the length of any singing, for sheer continual preparation to sing. Ottmar supported him; but, at the same time, considered that the introductory vision might be admitted to be Serapiontic; although, at the same time, Cyprian ought to be careful for the future not to dip into Ancient Chronicles, because reading of that sort was apt--as the present instance proved--to lead him into an unfamiliar province, in which-- not being native to the soil, nor endowed with a strong bump of locality--he wandered astray and lost himself, without being able to find the real path.

Cyprian, putting on a face of vexation, jumped hastily up, went to the fire, and was going to throw his manuscript into it. But Lothair went up to him, seized him by the shoulders, turned him about, and said with solemnity:

"Cyprian, Cyprian! withstand strenuously the foul fiend of author's pride, which, is vexing you, and whispering all manner of ugly things in your ear. I will address you in the formula of conjuration employed by the doughty Tobias von Ruelp, 'Come, come--tuck, tuck--it is contrary to all respectability, man, to play at pitch and toss with the Devil. Away with the ugly sweep!' Ha! your face lightens up! You are smiling! See what power over the demons I possess; and now I have some healing balm to drop upon the wounds, which your friends' adverse verdicts have inflicted. If

Ottmar thinks your introduction is Serapiontic, I may say as much for Klingsohr, and the fiery demon Nasias. Also the little automatic secretary strikes me as by no means lightly to be esteemed. If Theodore objects to the way in which you have portrayed Heinrich of Ofterdingen, at all events the suggestion of your portrait of him is to be found in Wagenseil. If he thinks it a fault that the singers never arrive at any actual singing from continual preparation for the same, I must confess that I do not quite know what he means. Perhaps he does not quite know, himself, what he means. I should scarcely think he would have wished you to introduce little verses of poetry, as being the masters' songs. The very fact of your not having done so, but left their words to our imaginations, redounds greatly to your credit in my opinion. I can never tolerate the introducing of verses into a story. They always seem to go along in it so lamely and limpingly, and interrupt its progress in an unnatural sort of manner. The writer--keenly impressed with the feebleness of his matter at some particular point--grasps at the crutch of verse. But if he manages, in this fashion, to prop himself along for a time, this sort of uniform, monotonous, tottery, pit-a-pat movement is very different from the firm tread of vigorous health; and, probably, it is a frequent error of our modern writers, that they seek their salvation exclusively in the outward, metrical form, forgetting that it is the poetic matter only which gives the metric pinions their due swing. Well-sounding verses have the power of inducing a species of somnambulistic intoxication; but this is very much like

74

the effect of the sound of a mill, or of other similar, regular and monotonous noises. They procure one a sound sleep. All this I merely say en passant, for the behoof of our musical Theodore, who is very often deluded ('bribed' was the word I was going to employ) by the sweet sound of meaningless verses; and, indeed, he is often attacked by a sort of 'sonnetical' mania, under the influence of which he brings into the world the strangest automaton-like little monsters. But now for you again, Cyprian. I do not think you ought to plume yourself much on your 'Singers' Contest.' I cannot say that I am altogether satisfied with it, though it certainly does not deserve death by fire. The laws of the land declare that abortions are not to be put to death if they have human heads; and in my opinion, this child of yours is not only not an abortion at all, but it is fairly well-shapen, though it may be a little weak about the limbs."

Cyprian pocketed his manuscript, and said, with a smile:

"My dear friends, you know my little peculiarity. When I get a little annoyed, because some fault is found with any of my feeble efforts, this is merely because I am so well aware how thoroughly the censure is deserved, and how much my productions merit it. Do not let us say another word on the subject of this story of mine."

After this the friends went back to the subject of Vincent, and his bent towards the marvellous. Cyprian's view was, that such a bent must of necessity be inherent in all poetic temperaments, and that this was why Jean Paul has said so many magnificent things on the subject of mesmerism, that a whole universe of hostile doubt would sink into insignificance in comparison with them; that poetical persons are the pet children of Nature, and that it is silly to suppose she can be displeased when those darlings of hers try to discover secrets which she has shrouded with her veil--as a fond mother hides from her children some valuable gift, only that she may afford them the greater pleasure by disclosing it to them.

"But, to speak practically," said Cyprian, "and this principally to please you, Ottmar: who that has looked carefully into the history of the human race--can have failed to be struck by the circumstance that, as soon as some disease makes its appearance like a ravening monster, Nature herself comes to the front with the weapons necessary to vanquish it; and, as soon as it has been overcome, another monster makes its appearance, with fresh powers of destruction; and new weapons are discovered again? And so goes on the everlasting contest which is a condition of the process of life--of the organic structure of the entire world. How if, in these times, when everything is spiritualized--when the interior relationship, the mysterious interdependence and interplay of the physical and psychical principles, are coming more and more clearly and importantly into evidence; when every bodily malady is found to have its corresponding expression in the psychic organism--how, I say, if mesmerism were the weapon--forged in the spirit--which Nature herself presents to us, as the means of combatting the evil which is located in the spirit?"

"Stay, stay!" cried Lothair, "where are we getting to? We

have talked far too much already on a subject which must always remain a foreign province for us; in which we can, at most, pluck for poetic purposes a few fruits, tempting by their colour and aroma; or transplant a pretty little tree or so into our poetic garden. I was delighted when Cyprian's story interrupted our wearisome discussion on this subject, and now we seem to be in danger of getting deeper into it than ever. Let us turn to something else. But wait a moment. First, I should like to give you a little 'pezzo' of our friend's mystical experiments, which I am sure you will enjoy. It is briefly this:--A considerable time ago I was invited to a little evening gathering, where our friend was, along with some others. I was detained by business, and did not arrive till very late. All the more surprised was I not to hear the very slightest sound as I came up to the door of the room. Could it be that nobody had been able to go? Thus cogitating, I gently opened the door. There sat Vincent, over against me, with the others, round a little table; and they were all staring, stiff and motionless like so many statues, in the profoundest silence, up at the ceiling. The lights were on a table at some distance, and nobody took any notice of me, I went nearer, full of amazement, and saw a glittering gold ring swinging backwards and forwards in the air, and presently beginning to move in circles. One and another then said, 'Wonderful!' 'Very wonderful!' 'Most inexplicable!' 'Curious thing!' etc. I could no longer contain myself, and cried out, 'For Heaven's sake, tell me what you are about?'

"At this they all jumped up. But Vincent cried, in that

shrill voice of his:

Recreant! obscure Nicodemus, coming slinking in like a sleep-walker, interrupting the most important and interesting experiments. Let me tell you that a phenomenon which the incredulous have, without a moment's hesitation, classed in the category of the fabulous has just been verified by the present company. We wished to try whether the pendulum-oscillations of a suspended ring could be controlled by the concentrated human will. I undertook to fix my will upon it; and thought steadfastly of circular-shaped oscillations. The ring--fixed to the ceiling by a silk thread--remained motionless for a very long time. But at last it began to swing, in an acute angle with reference to my position, and it was just beginning to swing in circles when you came in and interrupted us.'"

But what if it were not your will,' I said, so 'much as the draught of air when I opened the door, which set the contumacious ring in motion?'

Prosaic wretch!' cried Vincent: but everybody laughed."

"The pendulum-oscillations of rings drove me nearly crazy at one time," said Theodore. "Thus much is matter of absolute certainty, and any one can convince himself of it, that the oscillations of a plain gold ring, suspended by a fine thread over the palm of the hand held level, unquestionably take the direction which the unuttered will directs them to take. I cannot tell you how profoundly, and how eerily, this phenomenon affected me. I used to sit for hours at a time making the ring go swinging in the most various directions, as I willed it to do; and at last I went the length of making a regular oracle of it. I would say, in my mind, if such and such a thing is going to happen, the ring will swing in the direction between the little finger and the thumb; if it is not going to happen, it will swing at right angles to that direction, and so on.'"

"Delightful!" said Lothair, "you set up, within your own self, a higher spiritual principle, which, conjured up in mystic fashion by yourself, should make utterances to you. Here we have the true "spiritus familiaris," the socratic dæmon! from hence there is only a very short step to the region of ghost, and haunting stories, which might easily have their raison d'être in the influence of some exterior spiritual principle."

"And I mean to actually take this step," said Cyprian, "by telling you, on the spot, the most awful and terrible supernatural story I have ever heard of. The peculiarity of this story is, that it is amply vouched for by persons of credibility, and that the manner in which it has been brought to my knowledge, or recollection, has to do with the excited, or (if you prefer to say so) disordered condition which Lothair observed me to be in a short time ago."

Cyprian stood up; and, as was his habit when his mind was full of something, so that he had to take a little time to arrange his words in order to express it, he walked several times up and down the room. Presently he sat down, and began:--

"You may remember that some little time ago, just before the last campaign, I was paying a visit to Colonel Von P--

-- at his country house. The colonel was a good-tempered, jovial man, and his wife quietness and simpleness personified. At the time I speak of the son was away with the army, so that the family circle consisted, besides the colonel and his lady, of two daughters, and an elderly French lady, who was trying to persuade herself that she was fulfilling the duties of a species of governess though the young ladies appeared to be beyond the period of being "governessed." The elder of the two was a most lively and cheerful creature, vivacious even to ungovernability; not without plenty of brains, but so constituted that she could not go five yards without cutting at least three "entrechats." She sprung, in the same fashion, in her conversation, and in all that she did, restlessly from one thing to another. I myself have seen her, within the space of five minutes, work at needlework, read, draw, sing, and dance, or cry about her poor cousin who was killed in battle, one moment, and while the bitter tears were still in her eyes, burst into a splendid, infectious burst of laughter when the French-woman spilt the contents of her snuff-box over the pug, who at once began to sneeze frightfully, and the old lady cried, "Ah, che fatalita! Ah carino! Poverino!"

For she always spoke to the dog in Italian because he was born in Padua. Moreover, this young lady was the loveliest blonde ever seen, and, in all her odd caprices, full of the utmost charm, goodness, kindliness and attractiveness, so that, whether she would or no, she exerted the most irresistible charm over every one.

"The younger sister was the greatest possible contrast to

her (her name was Adelgunda). I strive in vain to find words
in which to express to you the extraordinary impression which
this girl produced upon me when first I saw her. Picture to
yourselves the most exquisite figure, and the most marvellously
beautiful face; but the cheeks and lips wear a deathly pallor,
and the figure moves gently, softly, slowly, with measured
steps; and then, when a low-toned word is heard from the
scarce opened lips and dies away in the spacious chamber,
one feels a sort of shudder of spectral awe; of course I soon
got over this eery feeling, and, when I managed to get her to
emerge from her deep self-absorbed condition and converse,
I was obliged to admit that the strangeness, the eeriness, was
only external, and by no means came from within. In the little
she said there displayed themselves a delicate womanliness,
a clear head, and a kindly disposition. There was not a trace
of over-excitability, though her melancholy smile, and her
glance, heavy as with tears, seemed to speak of some morbid
bodily condition producing a hostile influence on her mental
state. It struck me as very strange that the whole family, not
excepting the French lady, seemed to get into a state of much
anxiety as soon as any one began to talk to this girl, and
tried to interrupt the conversation, often breaking into it in
a very forced manner. But the most extraordinary thing of all
was that, as soon as it was eight o'clock in the evening, the
young lady was reminded, first by the French lady and then
by her mother, sister, and father, that it was time to go to her
room, just as little children are sent to bed that they may not
overtire themselves. The French lady went with her, so that

they neither of them ever appeared at supper, which was at nine o'clock. The lady of the house, probably remarking my surprise at those proceedings, threw out (by way of preventing indiscreet inquiries) a sort of sketchy statement to the effect that Adelgunda was in very poor health, that, particularly about nine in the evening, she was liable to feverish attacks, and that the doctors had ordered her to have complete rest at that time. I saw there must be more in the affair than this, though I could not imagine what it might be; and it was only this very day that I ascertained the terrible truth, and discovered what the events were which have wrecked the peace of that happy circle in the most frightful manner.

Adelgunda was at one time the most blooming, vigorous, cheerful creature to be seen. Her fourteenth birthday came, and a number of her friends and companions had been invited to spend it with her. They were all sitting in a circle in the shrubbery, laughing and amusing themselves, taking little heed that the evening was getting darker and darker, for the soft July breeze was blowing refreshingly, and they were just beginning thoroughly to enjoy themselves. In the magic twilight they set about all sorts of dances, pretending to be elves and woodland sprites. Adelgunda cried, "Listen, children! I shall go and appear to you as the White Lady whom our gardener used to tell us about so often while he was alive. But you must come to the bottom of the garden, where the old ruins are." She wrapped her white shawl round her, and went lightly dancing down the leafy alley, the girls following her, in full tide of laughter and fun. But Adelgunda had scarcely reached the old crumbling arches, when she suddenly stopped, and stood as if paralyzed in every limb. The castle clock struck nine.

"Look, look!" cried she, in a hollow voice of the deepest terror. "Don't you see it? the figure--close before me--stretching her hand out at me. Don't you see her?"

"The children saw nothing whatever; but terror came upon them, and they all ran away, except one, more courageous than the rest, who hastened up to Adelgunda, and was going to take her in her arms. But Adelgunda, turning pale as death, fell to the ground. At the screams of the other girl every body came hastening from the castle, and Adelgunda was carried in. At last she recovered from her faint, and, trembling all over, told them that as soon as she reached the ruins she saw an airy form, as if shrouded in mist, stretching its hand out towards her. Of course every one ascribed this vision to some deceptiveness of the twilight; and Adelgunda recovered from her alarm so completely that night that no further evil consequences were anticipated, and the whole affair was supposed to be at an end. However, it turned out altogether otherwise. The next evening, when the clock struck nine, Adelgunda sprung up, in the midst of the people about her, and cried--

"There she is! there she is. Don't you see her--just before me?"

Since that unlucky evening, Adelgunda declared that, as soon as the clock struck nine, the figure stood before her, remaining visible for several seconds, although no one but herself could see anything of it, or trace by any psychic sensation the proximity of an unknown spiritual principle. So that poor Adelgunda was thought to be out of her mind; and, in strange perversion of feeling, the family were ashamed of this condition of hers. I have told you already how she was dealt with in consequence. There was, of course, no lack of doctors, or of plans of treatment for ridding the poor soul of the "fixed idea," as people were pleased to term the apparition which she said she saw. But nothing had any effect; and she implored, with tears, that she might be left in peace, inasmuch as the form which, in its vague, uncertain traits, had nothing terrible or alarming about it, no longer caused her any fear; although, for a time after seeing it she felt as if her inner being and all her thoughts and ideas were turned out from her, and were hovering, bodiless, about, outside of her. At last the colonel made the acquaintance of a celebrated doctor, who had the reputation of being specially clever in the treatment of the mentally afflicted. When this doctor heard Adelgunda's story he laughed aloud, and said nothing could be easier than to cure a condition of the kind, which resulted solely from an over-excited imagination. The idea of the appearing of the spectre was so intimately associated with the striking of nine o'clock, that the mind could not dissociate them. So that all that was necessary was to effect this separation by external means; as to which there was no difficulty, as it was only necessary to deceive the patient as to the time, and let nine o'clock pass without her being aware of it. If the apparition did not then appear, she would be convinced, herself, that it was an illusion; and measures to give tone to the general system would be all that would then be necessary to complete the cure. This unfortunate advice was taken. One night all the clocks at the castle were put back an hour--the hollow, booming tower clock included-- so that, when Adelgunda awoke in the morning, she found herself an hour wrong in her time. When evening came, the family were assembled, as usual, in a cheerful corner room; no stranger was present, and the mother constrained herself to talk about all sorts of cheerful subjects. The colonel began (as was his habit, when in specially good humour) to carry on an encounter of wit with the old French lady, in which Augusta, the elder of the daughters, aided and abetted him. Everybody was laughing, and more full of enjoyment than ever. The clock on the wall struck eight (so that it was really nine o'clock) and Adelgunda fell back in her chair, pale as death; her work dropped from her hands; she rose, with a face of horror, stared before her into the empty part of the room, and murmured, in a hollow voice--

"What! an hour earlier! Don't you see it? Don't you see it? Right before me!"

Every one rose up in alarm. But as none of them saw the smallest vestige of anything, the colonel cried--

"Calm yourself, Adelgunda, there is nothing there! It is a vision of your brain, a deception of your fancy. We see nothing, nothing whatever; and if there really were a figure close to you we should see it as well as you! Calm yourself."

"Oh God!" cried Adelgunda, "they think I am out of my

mind. See! it is stretching out its long arm, it is making signs to me!"

And, as though she were acting under the influence of another, without exercise of her own will, with eyes fixed and staring, she put her hand back behind her, took up a plate which chanced to be on the table, held it out before her into vacancy, and let it go, and it went hovering about amongst the lookers on, and then deposited itself gently on the table. The mother and Augusta fainted; and these fainting fits were succeeded by violent nervous fever. The colonel forced himself to retain his self-control, but the profound impression which this extraordinary occurrence made on him was evident in his agitated and disturbed condition.

The French lady had fallen on her knees and prayed in silence with her face turned to the floor, and both she and Adelgunda remained free from evil consequences. The mother very soon died. Augusta survived the fever; but it would have been better had she died. She who, when I first saw her, was an embodiment of vigorous, magnificent youthful happiness, is now hopelessly insane, and that in a form which seems to me the most terrible and gruesome of all the forms of fixed idea ever heard of. For she thinks she is the invisible phantom which haunts Adelgunda; and therefore she avoids every one, or, at all events, refrains from speaking, or moving if anybody is present. She scarce dares to breathe, because she firmly believes that if she betrays her presence in any way every one will die. Doors are opened for her, and her food is set down, she slinks in and out, eats in secret, and so forth.

Can a more painful condition be imagined?

The colonel, in his pain and despair, followed the colours to the next campaign, and fell in the victorious engagement at W----. It is remarkable, most remarkable that, since then, Adelgunda has never seen the phantom. She nurses her sister with the utmost care, and the French lady helps her. Only this very day Sylvester told me that the uncle of these poor girls is here, taking the advice of our celebrated R----, as to the means of cure to be tried in Augusta's case. God grant that the cure may succeed, improbable as it seems.'"

When Cyprian finished, the friends all kept silence, looking meditatively before them. At last Lothair said,

"It is certainly a very terrible ghost story. I must admit it makes me shudder, although the incident of the hovering plate is rather trifling and childish."

"Not so fast, dear Lothair," Ottmar interrupted. "You know my views about ghost stories, and the manner in which I swagger towards visionaries; maintaining, as I do, that often as I have thrown down my glove to the spirit world, overweeningly enough, to enter the lists with me, it has never taken the trouble to punish me for my presumption and irreverence. But Cyprian's story suggests another consideration. Ghost stories may often be mere chimeras; but, whatever may have been at the bottom of Adelgunda's phantom, and the hovering plate, thus much is certain, that, on that evening, in the family of Colonel Von P---- there happened something which produced, in three of the persons present, such a shock to the system that the result was the death of one and the insanity of another; if we do not ascribe, at least indirectly, the colonel's death to it too. For I happen to remember that I heard from officers who were on the spot, that he suddenly dashed into the thick of the enemy's fire as if impelled by the furies. Then the incident of the plate differs so completely from anything in the ordinary mise en scene of supernatural stories. The hour when it happened is so remote from ordinary supernatural use and wont, and the thing so simple, that it is exactly in the very probability which the improbability of it thereby acquires that the gruesomeness of it lies for me. But if one were to assume that Adelgunda's imagination carried away, by its influence, those of her father, mother and sister--that it was only within her brain that the plate moved about--would not this vision of the imagination striking three people dead in a moment, like a shock of electricity, be the most terrible supernatural event imaginable?"

"Certainly," said Theodore, "and I share with you, Ottmar, your opinion that the very horror of the incident lies in its utter simpleness. I can imagine myself enduring, fairly well, the sudden alarm produced by some fearful apparition; but the weird actions of some invisible thing would infallibly drive me mad. The sense of the most utter, most helpless powerlessness must grind the spirit to dust. I remember that I could scarce resist the profound terror which made me afraid to sleep in my room alone, like a silly child, when I once read of an old musician who was haunted in a terrible manner for a long time (almost driving him out of his mind) by an invisible being which used to play on his piano in the night, compositions of the most extraordinary kind, with the power and the technique of the most accomplished master. He heard every note, saw the keys going up and down, but never any form of a player."

"Really," Cyprian said, "the way in which this class of subject is flourishing amongst us is becoming unendurable, I have admitted that the incident of that accursed plate produced the profoundest impression on me. Ottmar is right; if events are to be judged by their results, this is the most terrible supernatural story conceivable. Wherefore I pardon Cyprian's disturbed condition which he displayed earlier in the evening, and which has passed away considerably now. But not another word on the subject of supernatural horrors. I have seen a manuscript peeping for some time out of Ottmar's breast-pocket, as if craving for release; let him release it therefore."

"No, no," said Theodore, "the flood which has been rolling along in such stormy billows must be gently led away. I have a manuscript well adapted for that end, which some peculiar circumstances led to my writing at one time. Although it deals pretty largely with the mystical, and contains plenty of psychical marvels and strange hypotheses, it links itself on pretty closely to affairs of every-day life." He read: